CW01626821

Alien Vengeance

The Tactical Advantage Series – Book Three

Sean Patrick Posey

This is an original publication of Sean Patrick Posey.

This is a work of fiction. Names, characters, places and incidents either are the product of the author's imagination or are used fictitiously, and any resemblance to actual persons, living or dead, business establishments, events or locales, is entirely coincidental. The publisher does not have any control over and does not assume any responsibility for third-party websites or their content.

Text design by Sean Patrick Posey

3D Battle Carrier design by Sean Patrick Posey

3D Battle Carrier model by Sean Patrick Posey

Front cover design by Sean Patrick Posey

Front cover artwork by Sean Patrick Posey

FIRST EDITION: December 2019

Posey, Sean Patrick
Alien Vengeance/Sean Patrick Posey — First Edition

Science Fiction — Fiction

You can see other titles I have available on my website:

seanpatrickposey.com

ACKNOWLEDGMENTS

For Nicole, my sweet, beautiful, loving wife who encourages me to continue writing, and for my sweet beautiful daughters, Alyssa and Sarah, for whom I would do anything. I love you all.

TABLE OF CONTENTS

PROLOGUE

On their quest to become the most powerful species in the galaxy, the Xandurians created what some would say is the ultimate weapon, a time machine. Unable to match Earth's technology and military might in the here and now, their strategy is to travel back into the past and wipe out humanity in its infancy, erasing them throughout time.

In response, the Earth Defense Force sent a sizeable battle group into Xandurian space to destroy their time machine. The assault destroyed the time machine and the space station where it was being built. All the scientists working on the project were eliminated, and it was hoped that all data related to the time machine was destroyed, but there was no way to confirm this.

At the time of its destruction, the Xandurian time machine was complete except for one key element, it had no heart. The heart it needed was a simple hunk of rock. A hunk of rock only found on a small planet in the middle of Earth's space called Trynx 3. This special rock, an ore with temporal properties, would have enabled the machine to open a temporal vortex, making time travel possible.

Though the Earth Defense Force and Earth's Planetary Police were able to thwart several attempts by aliens to acquire a quantity of this ore, Earth's World Council concluded that it was only a matter of time.

The council decided it was far too dangerous to allow the ore to remain in existence, so they ordered the destruction of Trynx 3. The Earth Defense Force destroyed the planet in such a way that every speck of the ore and the planet was disintegrated.

CHAPTER 1 – DESTINY CHANGED

Captain Nathan Stone of Earth's Planetary Police Force has just begun a two day journey back to Earth from Jabrini 7. He and his crew spent the last six days tracking down a crew of four criminals, humans that deal in stolen weapons. They caught the criminals trying to break into an unmanned Earth Defense Force weapons storage facility. The criminals resisted. The confrontation ended badly for all four of them.

Shortly after jumping into FTL, Nathan's police cruiser's artificial intelligence, Vanessa, says, "Captain, there is an incoming transmission from Earth on the emergency channel."

Nathan stands up out of his chair and says, "On screen, Vanessa."

"Aye Captain."

The main view screen activates and then the president of Earth's World Council, James Siebert, appears sitting behind his desk in his office atop Earth World Council Tower in London, England. The look on the president's face instantly tells Nathan something's wrong. Something is very wrong. The pit of Nathan's stomach tightens up, and he braces for bad news.

"What is it, Mr. President? What's happened, sir?"

Speaking slower and in a lower tone than he normally would, the president says, "Captain Stone, at approximately 14:00 hours Pacific Standard Time today, an unknown enemy perpetrated an attack on both the Earth Defense Force headquarters and the Planetary Police headquarters in Seattle."

"What? How bad is it, Mr. President?"

"It's bad. Both buildings were reduced to piles of rubble in a matter of seconds. Reports are still coming in, but it appears that there are no survivors."

Feeling like he's just been kicked in the stomach, Nathan goes to sit down in his chair, but misses and hits the floor, his back landing against his chair. His gaze drops, staring at an empty spot on the floor. His mind fills with images of destroyed buildings, piles of rubble, and the faces of so many friends that may have been lost.

"You haven't heard the worst of it yet, Captain Stone. The senior admiralty was attending a conference on the top floor of EDF headquarters at the time of the attack. The Secretary of the Fleet, Admiral Hollister and Fleet Admiral Daniels included. They're all gone, Captain Stone."

Nathan doesn't react, he just continues to stare at the floor. He's not listening to the president, but everything the president has said registers in his subconscious.

"Captain Stone?"

Still no reaction.

The president tries a little louder, "Captain Stone?"

This time Nathan hears him and stands back up.

"Sorry, Mr. President."

"How soon can you get back to Earth?"

"We just left Jabrini 7, so we are still two days away at maximum speed."

"Very well, report to my office in London immediately upon your return. In the meantime, I'm sending you everything we have on the attack so far."

"Yes sir, Mr. President. Stone out."

Nathan pushes a button on the command console on his chair to end the transmission and says, "Vanessa, let me know when we have received the files from the president."

"Aye Captain."

The crew gathers around Nathan's chair to discuss what they have just heard.

The navigator, Mr. Black, says, "I can't believe it. Both headquarters leveled in a matter of seconds. All those people. How could this happen?"

With tears running down her cheeks, the tactical officer, Ms. Norata, says in a wavering voice, "All those people, our friends, our co-workers, all wiped out in an instant."

The helmsman, Mr. Bell, says, "It's so hard to believe. Who could have done this, Captain?"

"I can't be sure, but I have a sneaking suspicion the Xandurians are behind this attack. Vengeance for derailing their plan of taking over the galaxy. We'll know more once we examine the evidence. For now, back to your stations."

Everyone returns to their stations and their duties, but nobody is saying very much. Their hearts are heavy, and they are distracted. Their thoughts are of the friends and co-workers they may never see again, wondering if they have been killed in the attacks.

Snapping back to reality, Nathan realizes that the EDF and EPP headquarters might not be the only targets, so he decides to put his ship in defensive mode.

"Ms. Norata, raise the shields, bring the weapons systems online, engage the cloaking device, and rig for silent running. Keep your eyes on those long range sensors for any ships in our vicinity."

"Aye Captain, the shields are up, the weapons are online, I have engaged the cloaking device, and we are rigged for silent running. Long range sensors show no ships in this sector."

"Thank you, Ms. Norata."

A few minutes later Vanessa says, “Captain, we have received a large block of data in an encrypted message from President Siebert.”

“Very well, Vanessa, decrypt and display message contents.”

“Aye Captain, it will take about an hour to decrypt as there is a lot of data.”

“Okay, Vanessa. Let me know when it’s ready.”

“Aye Captain.”

The next hour goes by slowly and many thoughts are running through Nathan’s mind. Like most people it’s the not knowing that is bothering him the most. He is eager to see the data on the attacks. His thoughts also dwell on those that lost their lives in the attacks, what the future holds, and why President Siebert wants to see him.

Finally, after what seems like an eternity, Vanessa says, “Captain, I have finished decrypting the block of data from President Siebert.”

“Excellent, Vanessa, activate the main view screen and display all videos showing the attack on the EDF and Planetary Police headquarters.”

“Aye Captain.”

The main view screen activates and displays about a dozen videos that were captured by the city’s security surveillance system.

Nathan selects one video showing the Planetary Police headquarters. Approximately fifteen seconds into the video, there is a small flash of blue light above the building and then a cylindrical object suddenly appears in the sky.

The object appears to be rotating quickly on its vertical axis as it falls towards the building. As it gets closer to the building, it emits a thick, red particle beam straight down from an aperture on the bottom of the object. Immediately after that, the object emits what looks to be about a dozen long, red, plasma energy blades straight out to the side in a circular fan-like pattern. When the object reaches the building, there is no impact on the roof, the object falls right into the building. The thick red particle beam has burned a hole down through the center of the entire building. As the object falls through the building, the rotating energy blades slice the building into small chunks and send them falling towards the ground. It only takes a few seconds for the object to turn the entire building into a pile of rubble.

Nathan and his crew watch the video in disbelief. Never have they seen such a weapon take down such a large building in just a matter of seconds. Just when they think the attack is over the object self-destructs in a large explosion, startling everyone on the bridge, and sending building debris flying in all directions.

Mr. Black is the first to speak, "My God, that was unbelievable."

Mr. Bell says, "Nobody could have survived something like that."

Nathan says, "I agree, nobody could have survived that. Did that weapon look familiar to anyone?"

Ms. Norata says, "Yes, those blades looked a lot like the one on that prototype Xandurian ship we destroyed a few months back."

Nathan says, "Exactly. I'd bet my bottom dollar that weapon was Xandurian. This is exactly what I feared, the Xandurians haven't given up."

Nathan puts another video up on the main view screen that shows the same type of attack on the EDF headquarters building. It too was reduced to a pile of rubble in mere seconds, followed by a large explosion as the attacking object self-destructs.

Nathan says, "There is no doubt in my mind these attacks were perpetrated by the Xandurians. They couldn't go back in time to wipe us out in the past, so now they've declared war and are going to try it the old-fashioned way."

Ms. Norata says, "They would have to be insane to even try. Their ships are no match for ours, we've proven that several times. Plus, we destroyed most of their fleet a few months back. There's no way they've rebuilt it in such a short period of time."

Mr. Black says, "I agree, they would have to be crazy to even try to take us on in battle."

Nathan says, "Yes, so what are we missing here? What are they up to?"

"Ms. Norata, Mr. Black, I want you two to comb through the rest of the data that President Siebert sent us and see if you can find anything that can help to prove our theory."

Both Ms. Norata and Mr. Black answer with, "Aye Captain," and then dig into the other videos, the preliminary reports and the crime scene photos from both attacks.

Hours of digging through every file, picture and video that was sent reveals nothing that would point the finger at anyone else. Every scrap of evidence points to the Xandurians. Fragments of the metal casing from the devices chemically match the metal the Xandurians use for their ships' hulls. Several of the recovered components from the FTL drives used in the devices match components used in the FTL drives in the Xandurian warships. The devices were black with glowing green power conduits just like a Xandurian warship. All the characteristics of the red, plasma based, bladed energy weapons exactly match the weapon on the prototype ship that was destroyed a few months back. Also, the precise positioning when the devices dropped out of FTL is very reminiscent of how the prototype ship would drop out of FTL right on top of the target ship and slice it in half before the captain had time to raise their defenses.

The two day trip home to Earth is somber for Nathan and his crew. All of them are wondering about the future. What the

Xandurians have up their sleeves, what Earth's World Council will do to counter, and why President Siebert wants to see Nathan as soon as they get back.

As their police cruiser approaches Earth, a series of beeps comes from his console, and then Mr. Black says, "Captain, one minute until we arrive at Earth."

"Thank you, Mr. Black."

"Mr. Bell, drop us out of FTL."

"Aye Captain, dropping us out of FTL now."

The crew sees a bright blue flash of light through the bridge windows as the police cruiser drops out of FTL and the Earth instantly appears in front of them.

"Ms. Norata, disengage the cloaking device."

"Aye Captain, disengaging the cloaking device."

"Vanessa, contact Earth space flight control and get us clearance for re-entry. After that contact London air traffic control, request an approach vector and get us clearance to land on the helipad on top of Earth World Council Tower."

"Aye Captain."

A few minutes later Vanessa says, "Captain, Earth space flight control has granted us clearance for re-entry. London air traffic control has sent us an approach vector and granted us clearance for a vertical landing on the helipad at Earth World Council Tower. I have sent the approach vector to Mr. Black's console."

"Thank you, Vanessa."

Mr. Black reviews the data and says, "Confirmed, approach vector laid in, Captain."

"Thank you, Mr. Black."

"Mr. Bell, take us down."

"Aye Captain."

Mr. Bell noses the ship over and begins his descent into the atmosphere. The ship is descending over the Atlantic Ocean, approaching the west coast of England. As they approach Earth World Council Tower in London, Mr. Bell slows the ship down to a crawl and banks the ship to starboard slightly to line it up with the helipad. Soon the ship is hovering at two hundred feet directly over the helipad. Mr. Bell pulls back on the throttles and the ship descends slowly. When the ship has dropped to fifty feet, the landing gear comes down. A few moments later the wheels touch the ground and Mr. Bell shuts the engines down.

Nathan stands up and says, "Nice smooth landing, Mr. Bell."

"Thank you, Captain."

"All right everyone, shut everything down and let's go."

One by one they all exit the bridge and make their way down to the lower bay. Mr. Nagata, the ship's engineer, meets them in the lower bay. Nathan opens the ramp, and the crew walks out onto the helipad.

Nathan is the last one out and as he steps off the ramp says, "Vanessa, close and lock the ramp. Restricted access protocol."

Vanessa's voice comes over the external speakers, "Aye Captain, closing the ramp now. Restricted access protocol enabled."

Directly in front of the ship, across a short walkway, is the entrance to the building. The doors are made of glass, and Nathan and his crew can see two British Secret Service agents standing just inside, waving them over.

Nathan says, "All right, everyone, follow me," and then walks towards the glass doors.

As they enter, one agent says, "Captain Stone, we have been ordered to escort you and your party to President Siebert's office. Would you follow us please?"

"Lead the way, gentlemen."

The other agent walks over to the elevator and places his hand on a biometric hand scanner. The scanner turns green, a bar of white light runs from the tips of his fingers to the heel of his palm, and then displays a message that says, "Access Granted Agent David Hall."

The elevator doors open and everyone steps in. The agent pushes the button for the ninetieth floor, the doors close and the elevator begins its short descent, down two levels. When the doors open, they see four armed soldiers standing guard at the sliding glass doors that lead into the offices of the president and his staff.

The same agent walks over to the glass doors and places his hand on another biometric hand scanner. After scanning his hand, the scanner grants him access. The glass doors slide open and everyone walks into what looks like a reception area with a woman sitting behind a large, white and blue, curved desk. Behind her, on the wall, is a large video screen displaying the seal of the president of Earth.

The woman, dressed in a gray business suit, walks out from behind the desk with a tablet in her right hand. She is holding the tablet pressed against her chest.

She approaches the group and says, "Captain Stone, you and your party can follow me. I will take you in to see the president."

"Very well, lead the way."

The woman takes them down a short hallway to the right of her desk. She knocks on the door, opens it, and walks in. Over her shoulder, Nathan can see President Siebert sitting behind a large, antique wooden desk that is quite ornate. In front of his desk, imprinted on the navy-blue carpet, is another presidential seal. Mounted on the wall behind the president's desk is a row of large video screens displaying the city around the World Council Tower. Nathan assumes they have taken the place of actual windows for security reasons.

The woman says, "Mr. President, I have Captain Stone and party to see you, sir."

The president stands up and walks around in front of the desk while saying, "Yes, please come in, Captain Stone."

Nathan and his crew walk into the president's office and then the woman in the gray business suit exits the office, closing the door behind her.

Nathan reaches out to shake the president's hand and says, "It is an honor to meet you, Mr. President."

"Likewise, Captain Stone. I have heard many incredible things about you."

Nathan turns and motions toward his crew with his right hand and asks, "May I introduce my crew, Mr. President?"

"Of course, Captain Stone, I would love to meet your crew."

"Excellent, Mr. President, first we have my tactical officer, Aleena Norata."

The president shakes her hand and says, "A pleasure to meet you, Ms. Norata."

"The pleasure is all mine, Mr. President."

"Next we have my helmsman, James Bell."

The president shakes his hand and says, "A pleasure to meet you, Mr. Bell."

"Mr. President."

"Next we have my navigator, David Black."

The president shakes his hand and says, "A pleasure to meet you, Mr. Black."

"Mr. President."

"And finally, we have my chief engineer, Hiro Hashi Nagata."

The president shakes his hand and says, "A pleasure to meet you, Mr. Nagata."

"Mr. President."

The president motions with his right hand towards a sitting area with two large, white couches and two white armchairs over on the other side of his office and says, "Let's have a seat, shall we? We have a lot to discuss."

Nathan and his crew follow the president over to the sitting area and everyone takes a seat. Nathan's crew sit down on the couches, Nathan and the president sit down in the armchairs.

The president pulls open a small drawer in the table between the two armchairs and pulls out a box of cigars. He offers Nathan and his officers a cigar. They all politely decline. The president takes one and puts the box back in the drawer. He clips the end, lights the cigar and takes a long drag off it. The president pauses for a few seconds and then exhales the smoke.

With smoke tendrils swirling around his face the President says, "I'm sure you're all wondering why I've called you here so urgently, so let me get right to the point. Captain Stone, I'm recalling you to active duty in the Earth Defense Force and promoting you to the rank of fleet admiral."

Nathan's crew can't believe what they've just heard. All their jaws have dropped, their eyes are wide open and they're looking at each other in disbelief.

Nathan is stunned by what he has just heard and doesn't react at all. He's just staring blankly at the president. It takes a while before Nathan even blinks.

Finally, he asks, "I beg your pardon, Mr. President?"

"You heard me correctly, Captain Stone. I'm recalling you to active duty and promoting you to fleet admiral."

"But Mr. President, I served in the EDF for twenty-five years and retired. I work for the Planetary Police now."

"Yes, I know, Captain Stone, but circumstances have forced me to recall you to duty."

"What circumstances are those, Mr. President?"

The president takes another long drag off the cigar and exhales, smoke swirling up around his face, "The circumstances are that there is no one else, Captain Stone. The attack on EDF headquarters wiped out the senior admiralty and nobody else has your experience and knowledge. I need the 'living legend'. I need you, Captain Stone. Earth needs you."

Nathan sits there thinking for a minute and then asks, "Do I have a choice, Mr. President?"

The president smiles slightly and arrogantly says, "Not really, Captain Stone."

Nathan looks over at his crew who are all looking at him, waiting with bated breath for his response.

Nathan looks back at the president and says, "Very well, Mr. President, but I have two conditions."

"Name them."

"The first condition is I don't want to be sitting behind a desk, that's not me. I want my command back. I want the Invincible."

The president takes a quick drag off the cigar and exhales the smoke, "So, let me get this straight, Captain Stone. You want me to let my fleet admiral serve on the front lines? To be in combat and exposed to very real danger? My highest-ranking admiral, the man charged with leading the entire fleet?"

"Yes, Mr. President. I can't lead the fleet from behind a desk. I can't work that way. This is non negotiable. Take it or leave it, Mr. President."

"Okay then."

"Wait, what? That was too easy."

The president puffs out more smoke, “Oh, come now, Captain Stone, do you really think I don’t know what kind of man you are? I knew you wouldn’t agree to a position where you end up sitting behind a desk. Besides, I think you’ll be fairly safe on the bridge of a battle carrier surrounded by the most powerful ships in the known universe. What’s your second condition?”

“My second condition is I want my crew here with me. They all served under me on the Invincible before I retired, and I can’t imagine doing this without them.”

Nathan looks over at his crew as if to ask, “Are you in?”

All four of them look back at Nathan with a smile and nod.

The president smiles and says, “I think we can make that happen, Captain, or should I say, Admiral?”

Nathan and the president stand and shake hands, “Congratulations, Fleet Admiral Stone. In light of what’s happened, we’ll skip the pomp and circumstance of a swearing in ceremony.”

“Yes, of course, Mr. President.”

The president walks back to his desk, drops the cigar in an ash tray, opens a drawer and takes two things out. He walks back over to Nathan and says, “You’ll be needing these.”

The president hands him a set of black and gold five-star epaulettes and a set of gold insignia with five stars in a circle.

“I’ve taken the liberty of having new uniforms for all five of you delivered to your home in Jasper. They should be there waiting for you when you arrive.”

With a dumbfounded look on his face Nathan asks, “So you knew beforehand that I would agree to come back, that I would want my crew with me, and that they would agree to come back too?”

“That’s right.”

"How?"

Looking around at all of them the president says, "Let's just say that I know what type of people you are. Your core values include trustworthiness, patriotism, honor, duty and loyalty. Qualities that make you a little predictable, but they are qualities I look for in people."

"I think I speak for everyone here when I say, thank you, Mr. President."

The president nods at Nathan, turns to face the others and says, "Oh, I almost forgot, as a small reward for coming back to the Earth Defense Force to serve with Admiral Stone here, you four will be promoted two steps in rank."

"Ms. Norata, at the time that you left the EDF to follow Admiral Stone to the Planetary Police, you held the rank of lieutenant. You have been reinstated at the rank of commander. Congratulations, Commander Norata."

Ms. Norata smiles and says, "Thank you, Mr. President."

"Mr. Bell, at the time that you left the EDF you also held the rank of lieutenant. You have also been reinstated at the rank of commander. Congratulations, Commander Bell."

Mr. Bell smiles and says, "Thank you, Mr. President."

"Mr. Black, at the time that you left the EDF you were a Marine captain. You have been reinstated as a Marine lieutenant colonel. Congratulations, Lieutenant Colonel Black."

Mr. Black smiles and says, "Thank you, Mr. President."

"And finally, Mr. Nagata, at the time that you left the EDF you were a lieutenant junior grade. You have been reinstated as a lieutenant commander. Congratulations, Lieutenant Commander Nagata."

Mr. Nagata bows slightly and says, "Thank you, Mr. President."

"How about we celebrate your return to the EDF with a toast? I have an incredible fifty-year-old single malt scotch that is unbelievably smooth."

The president looks at each of his guests for a nod of approval. He gets one from each of them, even Ms. Norata.

The president smiles at her, almost in a lecherous way and says, "Well, well Ms. Norata, I'm impressed. Not too many women enjoy scotch, especially one as beautiful as you."

She smiles politely and says, "Thank you, Mr. President."

When the president turns to walk away, Nathan and Ms. Norata look at each other and Ms. Norata rolls her eyes, making Nathan smile and chuckle to himself.

The president walks over to the bar and pours six generous tumblers of the well-aged scotch and then delivers them, two at a time, to Nathan and his crew.

When everyone has their scotch, the president holds up his glass and says, "Gentlemen, and lady, to your return to the Earth Defense Force and to swift vengeance for those that we have lost."

The six of them clink their glasses together and take a sip of the scotch. Nathan and his crew are amazed, truly the best scotch they have ever tasted.

The President turns to Nathan and says, "Immediately after the attacks, I recalled every EDF warship to Earth. The Invincible is due to arrive in orbit tomorrow morning at approximately 09:00 hours. You will take command of her then."

"What about Admiral Jameson, Mr. President? He won't be happy about losing his command."

"I've already informed Admiral Jameson that you will be taking back command of the Invincible. He was disappointed until I informed him that his next command will be our newest, second-generation battle carrier, aptly named the

Vengeance, which was just completed last week. It's due to be commissioned and cleared for active duty once it completes space trials next week."

"You informed Admiral Jameson before I had even agreed to come back, Mr. President?"

Pointing at Nathan with his scotch glass, the president says, "As I said earlier, Admiral Stone, you're a little predictable."

Nathan downs the last of his scotch, puts his glass on the coffee table and says, "I'll have to work on being a little less predictable, Mr. President."

"I will leave that up to you, Admiral Stone. Now if you will excuse me, I have several urgent matters to attend to."

"Of course, Mr. President."

Nathan and the four members of his crew snap to attention and salute the president. The president returns the salute and then heads back to his desk.

Nathan and the others head back out the door they came in, the secret service agents escort them into the elevator and back up to the helipad. Nathan and his crew exit the building through the double glass doors and walk over to their police cruiser sitting on the helipad.

As they approach the front of the ship Nathan says, "Vanessa, unlock and open the lower ramp."

Vanessa's voice comes over the external speakers, "Aye Captain Stone, opening the lower ramp now."

Once open, everyone walks up the ramp into the ship and then they head up to the bridge. They all take their seats and prep the ship for takeoff.

When the ship is ready, Nathan says, "Vanessa, contact London air traffic control and request clearance for takeoff."

"Aye Captain."

"Mr. Black, plot a course for Jasper."

"Aye Captain."

"Mr. Bell, fire up the engines."

"Aye Captain."

The crew hears the jet engines spin up and start.

Moments later Vanessa says, "Captain, London air traffic control has granted us clearance for a vertical takeoff, no traffic in the immediate area."

"Thank you, Vanessa."

"Mr. Bell, take us home."

"Aye Captain."

Mr. Bell pushes the throttles halfway open, and the ship begins to rise. When the ship reaches two hundred feet, Mr. Bell adjusts the thrust vectoring, and the ship starts to move forward. Mr. Bell rams the throttles wide open after which the ship accelerates and climbs rapidly, pushing the crew back in their seats. In just a few minutes the ship is up at thirty thousand feet and cruising at five hundred knots.

"Captain, we have reached cruising altitude and speed, we should arrive in Jasper in approximately eight hours."

"Thank you, Mr. Bell. Increase speed to maximum. I'd like to get home to Jasper as soon as possible."

Mr. Bell says, "Aye sir," and pushes the throttles wide open.

The ship accelerates, and Mr. Bell calls out the air speed as it hits key levels, "Mach one, mach two, mach three, mach four, mach five........."

He continues until the ship stops accelerating at which point, he reports, "We have reached our maximum velocity of mach eight point five. At this speed we'll arrive in Jasper in approximately forty-five minutes."

"Excellent, thank you, Mr. Bell."

Half an hour later, a red light starts blinking on Mr. Bell's console indicating he has reached the point where he needs to decelerate so they can land in Jasper. He slows the ship down gradually over the next ten minutes until they reach five hundred knots.

Mr. Bell says, "Captain, five minutes until we reach Jasper."

"Thank you, Mr. Bell."

"Vanessa, contact Jasper air traffic control, request an approach vector and get us clearance to land on my helipad."

"Aye Captain."

A few moments later Vanessa says, "Jasper air traffic control has sent us an approach vector and granted us clearance for a vertical landing on your helipad. I have sent the approach vector to Mr. Black's console."

"Thank you, Vanessa."

Mr. Black reviews the data and says, "Confirmed, approach vector laid in, Captain."

"Thank you, Mr. Black."

"Mr. Bell, take us down."

"Aye Captain."

As they approach Nathan's home in Jasper, Mr. Bell slows the ship down to a crawl and lines it up with the helipad. Soon the ship is hovering at two hundred feet directly over the helipad beside Nathan's house. Mr. Bell pulls back on the throttles a little more and the ship descends slowly. When the ship has descended to fifty feet, the landing gear comes down. A few moments later the wheels touch the ground and Mr. Bell shuts the engines down.

Nathan says, "Nice smooth landing, Mr. Bell, as always."

"Thank you, Captain."

"All right everyone, shut everything down and let's go."

The crew finishes shutting down the ship's systems and then they make their way down to the lower bay. They open the ramp, walk out onto the helipad and then head into the house. One by one they grab a beer from the refrigerator in the kitchen and then head out onto the deck. When they get out on the deck, they find five good sized boxes sitting on the deck. The boxes are labeled with each crew members name and rank.

Nathan says, "These must be our new uniforms. The president is something else that's for sure. I wonder what he would have done if we had said no?"

Everyone chuckles at Nathan's last question.

After checking out the boxes, Ms. Norata raises her beer and says, "A toast to the newly appointed, Fleet Admiral, Nathan Stone."

The rest of the crew raise their beers and say, "Here here," then they all take a sip.

Nathan raises his beer and says, "Thank you, not just for the toast, but for your commitment and loyalty. It really means a lot to me."

Mr. Black raises his beer and says, "To the best damned commanding officer a soldier could ask for."

The rest of the crew raise their beers and say, "Here here," then they all take a sip.

Nathan raises his beer and says, "Thank you. Here's to the Invincible, our home for the foreseeable future. May she keep us safe and exact vengeance for our fallen friends."

The others raise their beers and say, "Here here," then they all take a sip.

Nathan raises his beer again and says, "Here's to all those that lost their lives in the attacks, may they rest in peace. I promise them all, that we will do whatever's necessary to find those responsible and make them pay."

The others raise their beers and say, “Here here,” then they all take a sip.

Nathan puts his beer on the table and grabs some wood to start a fire. The group sits around the fire for a few hours and enjoys a few more beers before they go inside and make dinner. After dinner they head into the theater room to watch an old science fiction movie. Nathan chooses a movie from the year 1978 called Battlestar Galactica.

“I think you’ll all like this one. It’s about a huge, heavily armed spaceship, from another part of the galaxy, that leaves on a mission to seek out Earth after their home planets are wiped out by their enemy in a sneak attack. I tried to watch it once, but I got interrupted and never got back to watching it.”

Nathan looks over at Ms. Norata who is already looking at him and smiling. Both remembering the “interruption” when Ms. Norata seduced Nathan for the first time a few months ago on the Aurora.

That is when it hits Nathan. He will have to end their intimate relationship. A high-ranking officer in the EDF cannot fraternize with a lower ranked officer, especially one serving under his command. Nathan and Ms. Norata are the only ones that know about their relationship. They decided to keep it a secret from the other crew members until the time was right, and that time never came.

After the movie finishes everyone heads to their bedrooms. A few minutes after Nathan gets in bed, before he turns the lights out, there is a knock at his door.

“Come in.”

The door opens and Ms. Norata walks in wearing a sexy, short, pink, satin robe. She walks up to the side of his bed, unties the robe and drops it on the floor, revealing a very sexy, see through, black, baby doll nightie that shows off her incredibly sexy body, leaving nothing to the imagination.

Nathan says, “Aleena…”

She puts her finger to his lips and says, “Shhhhh. I know what you are about to say. We aren’t actually back in the military until tomorrow morning, so we have all night to say goodbye.”

Nathan grabs her, pulls her into the bed with him, and kisses her. They spend the next few hours ravaging each other in every imaginable way, and then Ms. Norata heads back to her room so they can get some sleep. They have a big day ahead of them tomorrow.

CHAPTER 2 – BACK TO THE INVINCIBLE

The next morning, everyone meets in the kitchen at 07:00 hours. They all pitch in to make a huge breakfast consisting of scrambled eggs, bacon, sausage, toast, waffles, pancakes, hash browns, orange juice, and of course coffee. Everyone eats until they can't eat anymore.

They are all excited to be going back to serve aboard the Invincible. After breakfast they head to their rooms, pack their things and then help Nathan prepare the house and the hangar for an extended absence. When they have the house and the hangar all buttoned up, they put on their dress white uniforms, adorned with all their commendations and medals.

After getting dressed, Nathan takes a moment to look at himself in the mirror. He never thought he would be wearing the five gold stars on his shoulders and cuffs. Earlier in his military career, he dreamed of rising to the rank of fleet admiral, but as the years went on, he thought less and less about it. A feeling of great pride and accomplishment comes over him as he stares at those five gold stars.

When Nathan is done admiring himself in the mirror, he grabs his bags and heads outside. His crew is already on the helipad waiting for him, so he locks up the house and heads over to helipad. They walk up the ramp into the lower bay, closing the ramp behind them. They stow their bags in their cabins and then head up to the bridge to prep the ship for takeoff.

When the ship is ready, Nathan says, "Vanessa, contact Jasper air traffic control and request clearance for takeoff. Then contact Earth space flight control and get us clearance for space flight."

"Aye sir."

"Mr. Bell, fire up the engines."

"Aye Captain."

The crew hears the jet engines spin up and start.

Moments later Vanessa says, “Admiral, Jasper air traffic control has granted us clearance for a vertical takeoff and Earth space flight control has granted us clearance for space flight. Both report no traffic in the immediate area.”

“Thank you, Vanessa.”

“Okay, Mr. Bell, take us up.”

“Aye sir.”

Mr. Bell pushes the throttles half way open, and the ship begins to rise. When the ship reaches two hundred feet, he adjusts the thrust vectoring, and the ship starts to move forward. Mr. Bell rams the throttles wide open after which the ship accelerates and climbs rapidly, pushing the crew back in their seats. Several minutes after takeoff, the sky around the ship turns black as they near the edge of the planet’s atmosphere. At this point Mr. Bell disengages the jet engines and closes the air intakes. He then engages the sub-light engines and rams the throttles wide open. The ship accelerates, almost violently, to achieve escape velocity.

Vanessa announces, “Now leaving Earth’s gravity. Artificial gravity plating is coming online.”

As they break orbit Mr. Black says, “Admiral, I have the Invincible bearing two seven zero degrees at a distance of thirty thousand kilometers.”

“Very well, Mr. Black.”

“Mr. Bell, change course bearing two seven zero degrees. Take us to the Invincible.”

“Aye sir.”

As they get closer to the huge battle carrier, Nathan experiences a warm feeling in his core. The kind of feeling one gets when you see a loved one after a long time away, or the feeling one gets when you go home to see your family for the holidays.

Nathan smiles and says, "There she is, people. Isn't she a thing of beauty?"

Mr. Nagata says, "Aye sir, that she is."

A minute later Nathan says, "Vanessa, contact Invincible's air traffic control and request permission for a vertical landing on the elevator for shuttle bay alpha."

"Aye sir."

A minute later Vanessa says, "Admiral, Invincible's air traffic control has given us clearance for a vertical landing on the elevator for shuttle bay alpha."

"Thank you, Vanessa."

"Mr. Bell?"

"Yes, Admiral?"

"You heard the lady, put her down on the elevator for shuttle bay alpha."

With a big smile on his face Mr. Bell says, "Yes sir, my pleasure, sir."

The police cruiser is approaching the huge battle carrier from the port side a little low. As the ship rises above the flight deck of the battle carrier, Mr. Bell slowly circles the ship around, lines her up, lowers the landing gear, and sets the ship down gently in the center of the massive elevator. After that he shuts down the engines. Ten seconds later, the red strobe lights surrounding the elevator, light up and rotate. The atmospheric force field activates, and the elevator starts to lower the police cruiser into the shuttle bay.

As the tail of the police cruiser clears the flight deck, the huge shuttle bay doors above them begin to close. The crew looks out into the massive shuttle bay and the flurry of activity below them. When the elevator reaches the deck, a tug drives over, hooks up to the nose gear, and tows the police cruiser off the elevator. The tug then turns it around and backs it into one of the hangar bays. The ground crew quickly secures the police cruiser to the deck and then the tug disconnects and drives off.

The massive elevator rises back up towards the flight deck, the doors open as it approaches, and it locks in place with a loud metallic thud when it reaches the top.

After the crew finishes shutting the ship down, they head to their cabins, grab their bags, and then make their way down to the lower bay. They open the ramp and walk down onto the elevator.

As he reaches the edge of the ramp, Nathan says over his shoulder, "Vanessa, close and lock the ramp. Restricted access protocol."

Vanessa's voice comes over the external speakers, "Yes sir, closing the ramp now. Restricted access protocol enabled."

As he steps off the ramp onto the elevator, Nathan looks up and is surprised to see an ocean of dress white uniforms directly in front of him, with the senior officers out in front.

The Invincible's executive officer yells, "ATTENTION ON DECK," and everyone in the shuttle bay snaps to attention.

Over the PA speakers sounds a Bosun's whistle piping the notes to signify that the new commanding officer has come aboard. When the third pitch is played on the whistle, everyone in the shuttle bay salutes Nathan.

Nathan is shocked by this kind of welcome and takes a few seconds to process everything before he returns their salute.

It is really no surprise to the four other returning officers that so many of the crew lined up to welcome Nathan back as he was always very well respected and popular with the entire crew on the Invincible.

Nathan leads his four officers over to where the Invincible's senior officers are standing. Nathan walks up to and stands in front of Admiral Jameson. His officers line up to his left, slightly behind him. Nathan and Admiral Jameson salute each other and then shake hands.

Nathan says, "Admiral Jameson, I relieve you."

Admiral Jameson replies, "Admiral Stone, I stand relieved. Congratulations on being promoted to fleet admiral, sir. I can't think of a better man for the job."

"Thank you, I appreciate that, Admiral Jameson. Congratulations on getting the Vengeance as your next command. I hear the second-generation battle carrier is quite the ship."

"Thank you, Admiral. Now if you'll excuse me, I have a shuttle to catch."

"Of course, Admiral Jameson. Good luck and God speed."

The two admirals salute each other and then Admiral Jameson walks off across the shuttle bay.

The Invincible's executive officer yells, "CREW DISMISSED!"

Everyone in the formation disperses, many of them wait to welcome Nathan and his four officers back to the Invincible. After everyone has congratulated Nathan and welcomed the four former crew members back to the ship, the crowd disperses.

Nathan leads his people across the huge landing bay to the carrier's internal tram. They take the tram to the station under the carrier's island. After exiting the tram, they walk over to one of the three elevators. When everyone is in the elevator, Nathan pushes the buttons for levels forty and forty-two. When they reach level forty, which is designated for bridge officers, Nathan's four officers step out and walk down the corridor towards their cabins.

Nathan yells after them, "Get settled, get changed, and I'll see you on the bridge in half an hour."

The four of them yell back in unison, "Aye sir."

When the elevator reaches level forty-two, Nathan steps out and walks a short distance down the corridor to his state room. As he approaches the door, the ship's computer scans and identifies him, the door unlocks and slides open. Nathan stands in the doorway for a few seconds looking around his old state room. It hadn't changed a bit since he left the Invincible. It seems like only yesterday he retired from the EDF and left to join the Planetary Police.

As he steps inside and the door slides shut behind him, he feels a strange sensation, like he has just returned home.

After quickly unpacking and changing, Nathan heads back to the elevators and takes one up to level forty-five, which is the bridge level. When the elevator reaches level forty-five, Nathan walks out, turns to his left and approaches the large doors that secure the bridge. As he approaches, the ship's computer scans and identifies him, grants him access, and opens the large steel and glass doors.

The admiral stands just outside the open bridge doors for a minute taking in the high-tech beauty of the ship's command center. He had almost forgotten how cool the battle carrier's bridge is. Most of the bridge is adorned in a gloss white polycarbonate with some medium blue accents. There are also transparent section dividers and railings throughout the bridge. There are high-tech displays and touch screen control consoles at every station. All the displays and touch screen consoles have a high gloss black background with the control interfaces displayed in a medium to light blue color palette. There are several projected holographic displays operating throughout the bridge, including one at the tactical station and one at the navigation station. There is a combination of highly ergonomic, very comfortable, molded, seated stations that are manned continuously, and a few standing stations that are not. The outer bridge walls have a number of ten-foot-high by seven-foot-wide window sections, which have provided some spectacular views over the years. At the front of the bridge is a large view screen that retracts into the floor when not in use.

The design and color combination of the bridge truly is a thing of beauty.

After a minute the admiral snaps back to reality and steps onto the bridge.

As he steps foot on the bridge, the ship's computer announces in its female voice, "Admiral on deck."

Everyone on the bridge immediately stands and snaps to attention.

The admiral walks over to the command chair and sits down.

"At ease everyone."

Everyone takes their station again.

A few minutes later Ms. Norata, Mr. Bell, Mr. Black, and Mr. Nagata enter the bridge. Ms. Norata takes over the tactical station, Mr. Bell takes over the helm / navigation station, Mr. Black takes over the security station, and Mr. Nagata takes over the engineering station.

Through the bridge windows the crew can see hundreds of ships orbiting the planet. The president wasn't kidding when he said he had recalled the entire fleet home to Earth. It looks like most of it has already arrived.

"XO, has the whole fleet arrived home yet?"

"One moment, Admiral, I will check to see if we are still waiting for any ships to arrive."

The XO accesses the fleet arrival log from his computer console and then says, "Admiral, all ships are present and accounted for. The entire fleet is home."

"Thank you, XO."

Nathan turns his chair to look at his communications officer and says, "Comms, access the fleet assignments file I placed in your directory and send a copy of it to the commanding officer of every ship in the fleet. I'm splitting the fleet up into four large battle groups, each with a battle carrier and at least one dreadnought. That file will tell them which battle group they are assigned to."

"Aye sir, I have the file, sending it now."

"Thank you, Comms."

Nathan is just opening his mouth to give his next order when the communications officer interrupts him.

"Admiral, I am receiving a distress call, on the fleet emergency channel, from someone claiming to be the security chief on EDF Outpost 488. The problem is there is no Outpost 488, sir, I checked."

"On speakers, Comms."

Over the speakers comes a man's panicked voice, "Mayday, mayday, mayday. This is Lieutenant Michael Richards, security chief on Earth Defense Force Outpost 488. We are under attack. A small fleet of seven unidentified warships dropped out of FTL and opened fire without warning. The ships are black and green and shaped like giant angel fish. They took out our shields and weapons with the first few shots. I think they're preparing to board the outpost. Can anyone hear me? Please respond."

Nathan enters a query about Outpost 488 into the command console on his chair. His level of clearance is much higher than that of the communications officer, so the information on the outpost comes up for him. The computer asks for his authorization code to view the details about the outpost. Nathan types in his authorization code and scans the data on the outpost. When he gets about a third of the way down the screen, he reads something that makes an ice-cold wave travel down his spine, his adrenal gland goes into overdrive, and his heart rate jumps up.

Nathan's eyes open wide, he stands up briskly and says, "FUCK ME!"

"Comms, open a channel."

"Aye sir, channel open."

"Lieutenant Richards, this is Earth Defense Force Fleet Admiral Nathan Stone in orbit around Earth. We have received your distress call. We're on our way, just hold tight, we'll be there ASAP."

"Please hurry, Admiral Stone. They're sending over shuttles to board us."

"Understood. Stone Out."

The bridge crew can see that Nathan is more than a little panicked and are wondering what he just read about Outpost 488.

Nathan says, "Comms, send to all commands in battle group alpha. Go to battle stations, form up on the Invincible, set course for Saturn and engage their FTL drives, speed 3 TSL."

"Aye sir."

"XO, sound battle stations."

"Aye sir."

The XO grabs the microphone and announces over the ship's address system, "Battle stations, battle stations, all hands man your battle stations, this is not a drill."

An alarm sounds after his address and the lights on the bridge change from white to red.

After a minute or so the XO says, "Admiral, all sections report battle stations manned and ready."

"Thank you, XO."

"Tactical, has the battle group formed up on us yet?"

"Almost sir, thirty seconds."

"Helm, set course for Saturn."

"Aye sir, course plotted and laid in."

"Engage the FTL drive and take us to Saturn, speed 3 TSL."

"Aye sir, engaging FTL drive now."

The battle group, comprised of about eighty ships, accelerates rapidly away from Earth, each ship disappearing in a bright blue flash of light.

A minute later Mr. Bell says, "Admiral, we have reached 3 TSL and will arrive at Saturn in approximately two minutes forty-five seconds."

"Thank you, Helm."

"Comms, send to all commands in the battle group. As soon as they drop out of FTL, target any alien ships they see and open fire immediately. Destroy all targets. Don't wait for my orders."

"Aye sir."

Nathan turns, looks at Ms. Norata and says, "Did you hear that, Tactical? Open fire the second we drop out of FTL. Don't wait for my order."

"Aye sir."

The XO asks, "Admiral, can you tell us what's going on?"

"The Xandurians are attacking a super-secret storage facility hidden inside the giant gas body that is Saturn. That super-secret facility is where the EDF hid the working time machine we used to save Earth from the Sulari attack almost two years ago. I'm guessing they found its location by sifting through the classified information they acquired from the cybernetic organism they planted."

Nathan looks around the bridge at the faces of all the officers and all he sees is disbelief and fear. After seeing the looks on their faces Nathan decides to keep the final bit of information to himself. That being, the EDF stored a supply of the Trynx 3 time ore with the time machine as a "just in case" measure.

The Xandurians have found the one place where they can get everything they need to eliminate humans and become the dominant species in the galaxy. Nathan will be damned if he's going to let that happen on his watch.

About two minutes later a series of beeps comes from his console and then Mr. Bell says, "Admiral, thirty seconds to Saturn."

"Thank you, Helm."

"Tactical, anything on long range sensors?"

"Aye sir, I have seven targets locked. We are vectoring in on their starboard side aft, a little low. Perfect firing position, Admiral."

"Excellent, that's what I like to hear."

Ten seconds later Mr. Bell says, "Arriving at Saturn in 5… 4… 3… 2… 1…"

The crew sees a bright blue flash of light through the bridge windows and then Saturn instantly appears directly in front of the battle carrier. The Invincible is the first ship to arrive.

Immediately, Ms. Norata presses the fire button on her console. All the huge, front facing, laser cannon turrets on the battle carrier rotate slightly to port. The barrels raise up, taking aim at the Xandurian ships, and begin firing huge, red bolts of energy.

The seven Xandurian ships are only about five kilometers away. All seven ships are the same shape, they look like giant angel fish. They are all black with glowing green highlights on the leading edges of their hulls. One of the ships, in the center of the pack, is twice the size of the other six ships.

Nathan says, "Well, would you look at that? Looks like the Xandurians have built a new class of ship."

Two seconds later the rest of the battle group drops out of FTL, and immediately open fire with their massive laser cannon turrets. Literally thousands of huge, red laser blasts are being hurled towards the seven Xandurian ships.

As the first laser blasts impact the shields of the Xandurian ships, their sub-light thrusters begin to glow bright white and the ships slowly turn to face the EDF battle group head on. The Xandurians open fire with everything they've got, but it is pretty much a lost cause. The EDF's technology is far superior. The EDF's laser cannons are ten times more powerful and their shield technology is second to none. Nathan and the rest of the bridge crew watch as the Xandurian ships get pummeled by the massive barrage.

Nathan says, "These guys are crazy trying to stand toe to toe with us. The odds are more than ten to one."

Immediately after he finishes that sentence, two of the Xandurian ships' shields fail. The laser blasts begin blowing pieces of hull off the two ships. They are getting chewed to pieces and the impacts are knocking the ships off course. It's only a matter of time now.

A minute later the shields fail on the other four smaller Xandurian ships. Now they too are being chewed to pieces and knocked off course.

Twenty seconds later, the first two Xandurian ships explode and vanish in massive fireballs, huge chunks of the ship and smaller pieces of debris fly in all directions.

Thirty seconds after that, a third ship explodes, and then a fourth. A minute later, the fifth and sixth ships explode at the same time.

All that is left is the larger Xandurian ship, its shields are still up, and it's getting closer and closer to the EDF fleet. As a matter of fact, it's heading straight for the Invincible.

Nathan asks, "Does she intend to ram us?"

Ms. Norata replies, "She is definitely on a collision course, Admiral. One kilometer out and closing."

Nathan decides he doesn't want to play chicken with this insane Xandurian, so he says, "Helm, evasive maneuvers, drop us down, Z minus one thousand meters."

"Aye sir, evasive maneuvers, Z minus one thousand meters."

Mr. Bell fires the battle carrier's RCS thrusters and drops the massive battle carrier straight down, hoping they can drop quickly enough to avoid the collision.

"Tactical, tag that ship with a cloaked tracker, so we can track her if she jumps into FTL."

"Aye sir, firing tracker now."

Mr. Bell is successful in dropping the ship down quickly enough to avoid a collision. The large Xandurian ship cruises right through the line of EDF war ships, accelerates away rapidly, and disappears in a bright blue flash of light as it jumps into FTL.

Ms. Norata says, "Admiral, the enemy ship has jumped into FTL."

"Is the tracking device active?"

"Aye sir, the tracker is active, and the signal is coming in loud and clear. It looks like she is heading back to Xandurian space."

"Excellent, thank you, Tactical. I have a feeling we'll be seeing that ship again soon. I guess they've improved their shield technology because that ship took quite a pounding and we never cut through their shields."

"Comms, open a channel and get me Lieutenant Richards on the outpost."

A minute later the communications officer says, "Admiral, I have Lieutenant Richards for you."

"On speakers."

"Aye sir."

"Lieutenant Richards, this is Fleet Admiral Nathan Stone again. Can you read me?"

With laser blasts in the background, Lieutenant Richards answers in a hushed tone, "Yes, Admiral Stone, I read you."

"What is your situation, Lieutenant?"

"We have about a dozen armed aliens tearing the place apart. They're looking for something, but I'm not sure what. They've killed most of my security personnel and they've done a lot of damage to the outpost itself."

"Listen very carefully, Lieutenant. They're looking for the time machine that's stored somewhere in your facility. I'm sending a squad of Marines over to take care of the aliens, but until they arrive, I need you to do whatever you have to do to keep them from finding it. Understood?"

"Understood, Admiral."

"Excellent, hang tight, Lieutenant, the Marines are on their way. Stone out."

Nathan hits a button on the command console on his chair to close the channel. He gets up out of his chair and walks across to the other side of the bridge to speak to the Marine captain, Mr. Black.

"Colonel Black, do we have a number of the fourth generation armored exo-suits with special weapons packs and shields onboard?"

"Yes sir, we do indeed."

"Excellent. I want you to take two dozen Marines, in exo-suits, over to the outpost and secure it."

Mr. Black gets up out of his chair and says, "Aye sir," and then starts to leave the bridge.

Nathan turns and asks, "Mr. Black?"

Mr. Black turns back, looks at the admiral and says, "Yes, Admiral?"

"I don't want any Xandurians left alive. Understood?"

Mr. Black answers, "Understood, Admiral," then turns and walks off the bridge.

It takes Mr. Black about fifteen minutes to get the twenty-four Marines into the exo-suits, get them loaded on two shuttles and get the shuttles launched. Nathan is watching through the bridge windows as the two shuttles rise through the flight deck on the elevator for shuttle bay alpha. The shuttles lift off and head towards the planet. After just a few minutes flight time, they disappear into the giant ball of gas.

A few minutes later the communications officer says, "Admiral, I've just received a message from Colonel Black. He said they just landed in the outpost's shuttle bay, they've initiated their video streams and started their sweep."

"Thank you, Comms. Put their video feeds up on the main view screen."

"Aye sir."

The large main view screen activates and shows the twenty-four live video streams from each Marine's helmet cam. The bridge crew can hear Mr. Black giving his Marines their orders.

"Okay, listen up, Marines. We have twelve tangos to eliminate on this outpost. The life signs scanners in your suits will take you right to them. They will appear as the small red dots on your heads-up display. Power up your shields and select the plasma cannon from your weapons inventory. These Xandurians are tough and very aggressive, don't hesitate to fire, and shoot to kill. Split up into teams of two and get moving. Good hunting men."

The twelve teams of two all head off in different directions and go to different levels on the outpost. The Xandurians have done a lot of damage to the outpost. There is debris lying everywhere, there are wires, conduits and pieces of support structure hanging from the ceilings all through the corridors, and many of the lights are out. The ones that are still on are blinking on and off in an irregular pattern.

As the teams comb through the corridors of the outpost, they are running across members of the outpost's security team that have been killed by the invading aliens.

As the teams close in on the Xandurians, their vital signs monitors report that their heart rates and blood pressures are all rising.

Mr. Black's team is the first team to come in contact with a Xandurian. The alien jumps out from behind a large crate in the storeroom he was searching and opens fire on the two Marines. The shields on both Marines' suits take three blasts each before the Marines can react. The plasma cannon is mounted in the left arm of the fourth generation exo-suit. It is part of what is called the "special weapons pack" so it is not standard on all suits. Mr. Black is the first one to raise his left arm and return fire with his plasma cannon.

A large ball of what looks like liquid blue flame fires from the barrel on Mr. Black's left arm and streaks towards the Xandurian. The alien is not that far away from the Marines, so he has no time to dive out of the path of the blast. The large blue ball of energy hits the Xandurian square in the chest. The Xandurian's torso, upper arms and his thighs instantly liquefy and splatter blue goo all over the floor and nearby crates. The remaining chunks of him fly in all directions and end up spread out all over the floor in the storeroom.

Nathan yells, "YEAH, TAKE THAT YOU SON OF A BITCH!"

The communications officer was watching the feed from Mr. Black's helmet cam and says, "Ewwwwwwwwww, that's disgusting."

Both Nathan and Mr. Bell chuckle and then Nathan says, "Mr. Bell, do you remember on the Neptune One and on Lamaya 4, Mr. Black had Sulari and dragon worm guts splattered all over his suit's face shield?"

"Oh, yes sir, I remember. That was so damned funny."

"I've got ten bucks that says he ends up with Xandurian guts splattered all over him this time."

"I'll take that bet, sir."

"You're on, Mr. Bell."

One by one the teams of Marines find and eliminate the remaining Xandurians. The plasma cannons make short work of them but make quite a mess at the same time.

Mr. Black's team is approaching the last Xandurian's position. It is hiding somewhere in a large storeroom in the lowest level of the outpost. The two Marines enter the storeroom and wind their way through a maze of stacked crates and containers to where the heads-up displays in their helmets tell them the Xandurian is hiding, but when they get there, there is no Xandurian. They both stand there puzzled for a second, they look at each other and then turn in circles looking around. Neither of them sees anything and yet their life signs scanners are telling them they are right on top of it.

From above them, they hear a creak come from a large, wooden crate. Both men look up and raise their left arms to point the plasma cannons up towards the noise. A rather large Xandurian is perched on a corner of the large wooden crate and as the two Marines look up, it dives off at them. In reaction, both Marines fall backwards onto the floor and fire their plasma cannons. Both plasma discharges hit the Xandurian in the torso and instantly liquefy a large portion of his body. The blue goo splatters all over the exo-suits worn by the two Marines and cover them from head to toe. Their face shields and helmet cams are completely covered with the vile blue goo.

Nathan and Mr. Bell burst out laughing.

Mr. Black sits up and says, "God dammit, why does this always happen to me?"

Hearing this comment makes Nathan and Mr. Bell laugh even harder.

At that point Mr. Bell gets up out of his chair, walks over to Nathan, pulls a ten-dollar bill out of his pocket and slaps it into Nathan's hand. Mr. Bell shakes his head, heads back to his station and sits down.

Mr. Black and the second Marine start to wipe the blue goo off their face shields so they can see again.

Mr. Black says, "All teams, this is Colonel Black. All tangos are down, let's sweep the outpost for survivors."

The other Marines all acknowledge Mr. Black's order and begin a level by level, room by room search for anyone left alive. At the end of the two hour search, they've found five out of the twenty security personnel alive, including Lieutenant Richards. The Marines load the fifteen bodies of the deceased security personnel and the five survivors on the two shuttles and take them back to the Invincible. The bodies are taken to the ship's morgue, and the five survivors are taken to the medical bay to have their wounds treated.

Back on the bridge of the Invincible, Ms. Norata says, "Admiral, you better come and take a look at this."

Nathan gets out of his chair and walks over to the tactical station, "What have you got, Tactical?"

"My scans of the outpost show systems failure across the board. I don't think it has much longer."

"What's the time frame?"

"An hour, maybe two before total systems failure and then Saturn's gravity will pull it down and crush it."

"Thank you, Tactical."

"You're welcome, Admiral."

As Nathan turns to walk away and head back to his chair, he catches a look from Ms. Norata, a look of lust and wanting in her eyes from being close to him again. He pauses to let her know he noticed, and that's when her perfume registers. The sense of smell is one of the greatest memory triggers humans have. All kinds of memories flood into Nathan's mind, erotic images of Ms. Norata from their sexual adventures together. Ms. Norata can now see the same look of lust and wanting in Nathan's eyes, a look she has seen many times from him in the past few months. They smile at each other and then go back to their duties, hoping that nobody on the bridge saw their little exchange.

A short time later, Nathan gets up out of his chair and walks towards the large glass and steel doors at the back of the bridge, which open as he approaches.

As he exits, he says, "XO, you have the con."

"Aye sir."

Nathan takes an elevator down to the medical bay to speak to Lieutenant Richards. When Nathan walks in, he finds Lieutenant Richards sitting on one of the beds having some nasty cuts sealed up on his forehead and on his arms.

Nathan says, "Lieutenant Richards, I'm Admiral Stone. How are you holding up?"

"Nice to meet you, Admiral Stone. Considering the circumstances, I would say I'm doing pretty well, thank you. I only have a few cuts and bruises. It could have been a lot worse."

"Indeed, Lieutenant."

"Thank you for the rescue, Admiral. Me and the others appreciate you getting here so quickly."

"You're very welcome, Lieutenant."

"Excuse me for saying this, sir, but I'm guessing that checking up on me and my men is not the only reason you came down here."

"You would be correct, Lieutenant. I have some bad news about your outpost. The Xandurians did a lot of damage when they were rampaging through looking for the time machine.

Almost all the primary systems are offline and several of the backup systems are failing."

"How long?"

"An hour, maybe two before the stability systems fail and the outpost gets sucked down by Saturn's gravity."

"What do you need from me, Admiral?"

"I need your help to retrieve the time machine and the Trynx 3 ore before we lose the outpost. Is there anything else we should retrieve besides the time machine?"

"Nothing comes to mind, Admiral. Most of what is stored on the outpost are classified projects that failed. They decided to store them instead of destroying them just in case they could be utilized in some way in the future."

"Very well, Lieutenant, there is a cargo shuttle waiting for you in shuttle bay alpha. I suggest you hurry."

"Aye sir."

Nathan heads back to the elevators and takes one back up to the bridge.

When the doctor has finished treating his minor wounds, Lieutenant Richards heads for the shuttle bay. When the lieutenant reaches the shuttle bay, he spots the cargo shuttle sitting on the elevator and four crewmen standing at the end of the rear loading ramp. The lieutenant joins the four waiting crewmen, they board the shuttle and close the ramp.

Everyone takes their seats and the pilot powers up the shuttle. The elevator the shuttle is on begins to rise, the atmospheric force field activates, and the large elevator doors above them begin to open. When the elevator reaches the flight deck, the shuttle pilot gets clearance from Invincible's air traffic control to depart, so the shuttle lifts off the deck and turns to head towards the planet.

Nathan walks over to the front bridge windows and watches with angst as the cargo shuttle takes off towards Saturn. The stability systems could fail at any time so he hopes that the men can get in, grab the time machine, and get out before that happens.

After just a few minutes flight time, they disappear into the giant ball of gas. A few minutes later, the shuttle lands in the outpost's shuttle bay and the pilot shuts the engines down. One of the crewmen opens the rear loading ramp and the five of them exit the shuttle. Lieutenant Richards leads the four crewmen down two levels to the high security vault that was installed specifically for the time machine. The lieutenant opens the vault using his security code and when the thick steel door swings open. The only thing the men see inside is one fairly large crate sitting all by itself in the middle of the large vault. The five men bring the crate containing the time machine to the cargo elevator using an anti-gravity hand truck. They take the elevator back to the shuttle bay and then load the crate into the rear bay of the cargo shuttle.

After securing the precious cargo, they close the rear loading ramp and take their seats. The pilot powers up the shuttle and lifts off. A few minutes later the shuttle clears the giant ball of gas and starts the short flight back to the Invincible.

When Nathan sees the shuttle emerge from Saturn, he breathes a huge sigh of relief. Mission accomplished, and everyone is safely off the doomed outpost. Nathan walks over to the port side bridge windows to watch the shuttle approach the carrier, fly in over the flight deck, and land on the elevator for shuttle bay alpha.

As the shuttle is lowered into the shuttle bay, the large glass and steel bridge doors open, and in walks Mr. Black.

As Mr. Black sits down in his chair, Nathan turns toward him and says, "Great job clearing the outpost, Colonel Black, outstanding work."

"Thank you, Admiral."

Nathan turns and then turns back with a smile on his face, "Oh, and great job getting splattered head to toe with alien goo once again. You're three for three. Consistency is an admirable quality in an officer."

Mr. Black smiles, drops his head in embarrassment and shakes it from side to side while thinking to himself, "I knew it. I'm never going to live that down."

The rest of the bridge crew has a good chuckle over Nathan's comment and Mr. Black's embarrassment.

After the laughter dies down, Nathan decides to go down to the shuttle bay to greet the returning team. He pauses for a moment as an idea pops into his head.

He turns to face the engineering station and says, "Mr. Nagata, would you accompany me to the shuttle bay please?"

"Of course, Admiral."

The two men exit the bridge through the large glass and steel doors, which open as they approach, and take an elevator down to the carrier's internal tram.

There is a tram sitting there waiting when they exit the elevator, so they walk right on and Nathan touches shuttle bay alpha on the tram's diagram. The doors close, the tram begins to move and is soon traveling quite quickly.

"Mr. Nagata, I sent a team back to the outpost to retrieve the time machine and they have just landed in the shuttle bay. I would like you to take the time machine down and connect it to the reactors and shield emitters, then install the control console on the bridge next to my station."

"Admiral, do you think that is wise? Wouldn't the time machine be safer somewhere else?"

"In my opinion there is no place safer than one of the most secure sections of a battle carrier surrounded by the entire EDF fleet."

"That may be true, Admiral, but why install it? You can't be thinking of using it? I respectfully remind the Admiral that time travel can be extremely dangerous."

"I agree, Mr. Nagata, but it is better to be prepared for anything. I would rather have it at my disposal at a moment's notice when needed, than miss what could be my only opportunity to save humanity. Don't you agree?"

"I can see your point, Admiral, but it is still a very dangerous machine to have at your fingertips."

Before too long, the tram begins to slow down and pulls into the stop in shuttle bay alpha. Nathan and Mr. Nagata step off the tram and walk over to the cargo shuttle sitting on the elevator. As they approach, they see that the four crewmen and Lieutenant Richards are bringing the crate down the rear loading ramp of the cargo shuttle.

Nathan says, "Great job retrieving the time machine, gentlemen."

All five men answer, "Thank you, Admiral."

"Now if you will all follow Commander Nagata, he will show you where the time machine needs to go. Thank you, gentlemen."

All five men answer, "Aye sir."

Mr. Nagata says, "Okay, gentlemen, we're heading for the reactor room," and then he leads them over to the cargo elevators where they load the crate and take the elevator down.

Nathan heads across the huge landing bay to the internal tram and takes it to the station under the carrier's island. After exiting the tram, he walks over to one of the three elevators. He walks into one and pushes the button for level forty-five, the bridge.

On the ride up to the bridge, Nathan, being very thorough, decides he needs to make sure that everything on the outpost and the outpost itself is destroyed. He doesn't want to leave any possibility of any technology falling into the wrong hands.

When the elevator reaches level forty-five, Nathan walks out, turns to his left and approaches the large doors that secure the bridge. As he approaches, the ship's computer scans and identifies him, grants him access, and opens the large steel and glass doors.

As Nathan enters the bridge he says, "Tactical, arm a dozen mark four ship to ship missiles, target the outpost and fire when ready."

"Aye sir, arming missiles, target acquired, firing."

At six locations around the battle carrier's island superstructure, missile bay doors open, missile launchers rise up and spin, so they face in the direction of the outpost, and launch two missiles each.

The missiles streak towards Saturn in a large arc and then disappear into the giant ball of gas. The outpost is a couple of miles down into the gas, so it takes the missiles a minute to reach it.

Ms. Norata says, "Missiles are approaching the target. Impact in 5... 4... 3... 2... 1... now."

Several bright white flashes of light appear through the gas as the missiles detonate.

Ms. Norata says, "Admiral, my scans confirm the target has been destroyed and Saturn's gravity is pulling the debris down."

"Thank you, Tactical."

"Comms, send to all commands in the battle group. Stand down from battle stations, form up on the Invincible, set course for Earth and engage their FTL drives, speed 3 TSL."

"Aye sir."

"XO, stand down from battle stations."

"Aye sir.

The XO grabs the microphone and announces over the ship's address system, "Attention all hands, stand down from battle stations, repeat stand down from battle stations."

A chime sounds after his address and the lights on the bridge change from red to white.

"Helm, set course for Earth."

"Aye sir, course plotted and laid in."

"Engage the FTL drive and take us to Earth, speed 3 TSL."

"Aye sir, engaging FTL drive now."

The battle group accelerates rapidly away from Saturn, each ship disappearing in a bright blue flash of light.

A minute later Mr. Bell says, "Admiral, we have reached 3 TSL and will arrive at Earth in approximately two minutes forty-five seconds."

"Thank you, Helm."

About two minutes later a series of beeps comes from his console and then Mr. Bell, says, "Admiral, thirty seconds to Earth."

"Thank you, Helm."

Twenty-five seconds later Mr. Bell says, "Arriving at Earth in 5... 4... 3... 2... 1..."

The crew sees a bright blue flash of light through the bridge windows and then Earth and the rest of the EDF fleet instantly appear directly in front of the battle carrier.

Nathan says, "Comms, get me President Siebert please."

"Aye sir."

A few minutes later the communications officer says, "Admiral, I have President Siebert for you, sir."

"Thank you, Comms, on screen please."

"Aye sir."

The main view screen activates, and President Siebert appears sitting behind his desk in his office atop Earth World Council Tower in London, England.

"Fleet Admiral Stone, to what do I owe this pleasure?"

"Mr. President, I'm calling to inform you that my battle group has just returned from Saturn where we stopped the Xandurians from stealing our functioning time machine and a supply of the Trynx 3 ore from a top-secret storage facility hidden a few miles down inside the gas of Saturn itself."

"What? They dared to launch an attack so close to Earth with our entire fleet in orbit? Are they mad?"

"I can't say for sure, Mr. President, but I would say they are desperate. It seems they are willing to do just about anything to achieve their goal of destroying us and becoming the most powerful species in the galaxy."

"I would have to agree with you, Admiral Stone. I will call an emergency meeting of the council to discuss what we should do about the continuing Xandurian threat. In the meantime, what have you done with the time machine?"

"Mr. President, I am keeping the time machine aboard the Invincible and have instructed my chief engineer to take it down to our reactor room and hook it up to our reactors and the shield emitters."

"Don't you think it's dangerous to have the time machine on board, out in the open like that? Shouldn't we hide it away somewhere safe?"

"With all due respect, Mr. President, we had it hidden away somewhere safe. The Xandurians found it and tried to steal it from our most top-secret facility. Right now, I can't think of a safer place to keep it than in the center of a battle carrier surrounded by our entire fleet. I'd like to see them try to take it from us now."

"I see your point, Admiral Stone. May I ask why are you having your chief engineer install it? Are you thinking of using it? Do I have to remind you that time travel can be extremely dangerous?"

"No need to remind me, Mr. President, I'm well aware of the danger. As I told my chief engineer, it is better to be prepared for anything. I would rather have it at my disposal at a moment's notice when needed, than miss what could be my only opportunity to save humanity. Don't you agree, Mr. President?"

"I can see your point, Admiral, but it is still a very dangerous machine to have at your fingertips. It is not to be taken lightly, Admiral Stone."

"Funny, that's the same thing my chief engineer said. My answer to you, Mr. President, is I have many extremely powerful weapons at my disposal, and I don't take any of them or my responsibilities lightly."

"Well, when you put it that way, Admiral. I'll contact you again after the council meeting."

"Very well, Mr. President. Stone out."

Nathan pushes a button on the command console on his chair to end the transmission and shut down the main view screen.

It is now late in the afternoon aboard the Invincible. Nathan has a meeting with the department heads to go over carrier operations. Following that, his duty shift over, he heads down to his private dining room for dinner.

As he enters, he is greeted by his personal chef, the very same chef from two years ago when Nathan commanded the Invincible.

The chef reaches out, shakes Nathan's hand and says, "Admiral Stone, it is a real pleasure to see you again, sir. Welcome back to the Invincible. I was happy to hear that you were returning."

"Thank you for the warm welcome, Chef, I appreciate it. I'm happy to see you again as well. How have you been? Everything good at home with the family?"

"I'm doing just fine, thank you, Admiral. Yes, everything is good at home. My wife is well, and my kids are growing like crazy."

"Glad to hear it, Chef. Make sure to tell your wife that I say hello."

"I will, sir. Now, I have prepared a special dinner tonight to welcome you back to the Invincible. I made all your favorites starting with French onion soup, for the entrée I have a nice thick fillet steak Oscar, cooked medium rare and a nice big Atlantic lobster tail. For sides I have a garden salad, garlic mashed potatoes, a vegetable medley and a couple of slices of garlic bread."

"It all sounds delicious, Chef, thank you. I don't know if I'll be able to eat all of that, but I'll do my best."

"Of course, sir, it'll just be a few minutes and I'll bring out your soup. I've already poured you a scotch, it's on the table so just sit down, relax and enjoy."

"Excellent, thank you, Chef."

"It's my pleasure, sir."

The chef disappears into the kitchen and Nathan sits down at the table. He picks up the scotch, sniffs it and takes a good sip. He activates the holographic display at the center of his dining table and looks through the ship's logs while he waits.

Over the next hour and a half Nathan eats the amazing dinner the chef has prepared for him. When he is finished and can't possibly eat anymore, he decides to head back to his state room.

Before he leaves the dining room, the chef comes out and says, "I hope you enjoyed dinner, Admiral."

"Chef, it was incredible. I can't thank you enough."

“You are welcome, sir. Have a good night, Admiral.”

“You too, Chef.”

Nathan turns and exits the dining room and walks down the corridor to his state room. As he approaches the door, the ship’s computer scans and identifies him, after which the door slides open. As he steps inside, and the door slides shut behind him.

Nathan pours himself another scotch, sits down on the couch in the living area and puts on an old science fiction movie. Two hours and several scotches later he decides to have a nice, long, hot, relaxing shower and go to bed.

After his shower, while brushing his teeth, someone rings the door chime. He quickly rinses his mouth out, throws a towel around his waist and walks over to the door.

CHAPTER 3 – BREAKING REGULATIONS

As Nathan approaches, the gray metal door slides open. To Nathan's surprise he sees Ms. Norata standing in the corridor.

She looks Nathan up and down and smiles because she likes what she sees. Her skin goes flush and the look on her face turns to one of pure lust.

Nathan notices that her hair is down, her makeup looks freshly applied, and she is wearing a gray zippered flight suit style uniform that they wear on a mission, not when they are off duty. This flight suit is tight and form fitting, showing off Ms. Norata's ample curves and the zipper in the front is pulled down just enough to show a hint of her incredible cleavage. Nathan feels the excitement build in his stomach, his heart rate spikes, his blood moves south, and he feels his erection begin to form.

After a few seconds of awkward silence Nathan says, "Ms. Norata, what can I do for you?"

"I have something to discuss with you, Admiral. May I come in?"

Nathan ponders for a second if inviting her in would be appropriate, given their ranks, and then says, "Yes, of course, come in, Ms. Norata."

Ms. Norata enters Nathan's state room and the door slides closed behind her.

Nathan turns and walks away from her saying, "Give me a minute to throw some clothes on and then we can talk."

Ms. Norata says, "Oh, don't get dressed on my account. Here, let me join you."

Nathan turns, after hearing this, to see Ms. Norata pulling the front zipper on her flight suit all the way down. She pulls her arms out of the sleeves and drops the flight suit on the floor.

Nathan is speechless as his eyes take in the beautiful, sexy woman standing in front of him dressed only in a pair of white lace bikini panties, a white lace push-up bra and a set of high heels, which he didn't notice she had on until she undressed.

Many thoughts are running through Nathan's mind. Part of his brain is saying you can't do this because it's against regulations. The other part of his brain is remembering that Ms. Norata is like a wild animal in bed and their sexual adventures together were like nothing he had ever experienced before. Of course, Nathan's decision-making ability may be a little compromised due to the fact his brain is swimming in scotch.

With a lustful little grin on her face, Ms. Norata steps out of her flight suit and walks slowly towards Nathan, seductively swinging her hips from side to side. She never takes her eyes off his. When she reaches Nathan, she grabs the front of his towel and pulls it off, dropping it on the floor.

Nathan's large erection springs out and up, right into Ms. Norata's hand. She wraps her hand around it and begins stroking it gently, never breaking eye contact.

Nathan begins to say, "Ms. Norata..., Aleena, we can't..."

Ms. Norata cuts him off and says, "Are you sure about that? Part of you really wants to, that's for sure."

Nathan says nothing else, so Ms. Norata drops to her knees, takes his large erection in both hands and engulfs the rest with her mouth. She then removes one of her hands and works more and more of it into her mouth. Soon after, she removes her other hand and takes his entire length into her mouth and down her throat.

Nathan gasps out loud as Ms. Norata swallows him whole. It always amazes Nathan that she can take all of him down her throat. She is the only woman that has ever done that to Nathan because of his size. Her warm mouth and throat feel incredible.

Ms. Norata pleasures Nathan this way for the next five minutes. Nathan is enjoying what she is doing immensely, but he is looking forward to pleasuring her.

The next time she comes up for air Nathan, picks her up and carries her into the bedroom. He places her on her back on the bed and then kneels down before her.

She knows what he wants, and she wants it too. She pulls her knees up and spreads her thighs apart for him.

Nathan grabs the edge of her panties, pulls them aside and buries his tongue inside her.

Ms. Norata gasps at the intense pleasure. She grabs handfuls of his hair and pulls him into her.

Nathan pulls back just a little and finds that special little spot with his tongue.

Ms. Norata instantly explodes, a very intense orgasm wracks her body, causing her to spasm uncontrollably.

Nathan doesn't give her any time to recover from that intense orgasm. While she is still in orgasm, he stands up between her legs, pulls her panties aside again and drives his large erection deep inside her.

Ms. Norata gasps loudly from the sudden intrusion and from Nathan's size.

Nathan gives her a few seconds to get used to his size before he pulls almost all the way out and then thrusts all the way back inside her.

Ms. Norata lets out a long sensual moan.

Ms. Norata has always loved Nathan to take her hard, rough, and fast so Nathan takes both of her hands in his left hand and pins them on the bed above her head. He then wraps his right hand around her throat and squeezes slightly.

He lowers his lips to hers and kisses her hard, at the same time he pulls back and rams himself into her as hard as he can.

Ms. Norata cries out into Nathan's mouth.

Nathan continues to ram himself into her, increasing his pace until he is ramming into her as hard, rough, and fast as he can. Nathan keeps his mouth clamped over hers to keep her screams muffled, but with the intensity of his assault, he needs to break his kiss to breathe through his mouth.

To keep her quiet, he pulls his right hand from her throat and clamps it tightly over her mouth.

Ms. Norata screams loudly into Nathan's hand as he continues to ravage her. She has reached orgasm again, but this one is not stopping. As Nathan continues pounding into her, she is experiencing one long, intense orgasm.

The excitement is too much for Nathan, he thrusts into her one last time as he explodes deep inside her. He collapses on top of her, exhausted from both the physical activity and a very intense orgasm.

Nathan finally catches his breath and says, "Oh my God Aleena, that was incredible. I miss you so much."

Ms. Norata can't answer him yet, she is still recovering from her orgasm.

After recovering from their first session, Nathan picks her up and carries her across the room. He bends her over the back of the couch, kicks her feet apart and takes her hard, rough, and fast from behind. He clamps one hand firmly over her mouth while his other hand plays with her large, firm breasts.

It doesn't take either of them long to reach orgasm.

When they have recovered from their second session, Aleena takes control. She guides him back to the bed, pushes him down on it and then climbs on top of him. She puts her amazing breasts in his face, grips his large erection with her small hand and then slides it deep inside herself. She rides Nathan and grinds into him through three more orgasms before collapsing on top of him, exhausted.

Nathan lets Aleena recover for a few minutes and then suggests they take a shower together. After getting in the nice, hot shower, they soap each other up.

It doesn't take long before Nathan is fully erect again. Nathan picks Aleena up and places her back against the wall of the shower.

Aleena wraps her arms and legs around him and Nathan thrusts deep inside of her.

He places his mouth over hers to keep her quiet and takes her with long slow strokes, slowly increasing his pace until he is ravaging her like an animal once again.

Aleena screams into his mouth while he brings her to four more orgasms before he explodes deep inside her.

After their shower, they are exhausted. They both need to get some sleep as their duty shifts start early in the morning.

Aleena puts her clothes back on and Nathan puts on a pair of track pants and a t-shirt.

After they get dressed, Nathan walks her over to his stateroom door.

He has her stay back in the room a little bit, while he opens the door and looks around. There is nobody in the corridor, so he motions to Aleena to come to the door and that the coast is clear.

Aleena walks out, giving Nathan a quick kiss as she exits his stateroom and says, "We have to do this again soon."

Aleena walks away down the corridor and Nathan can't help but stare at her amazing backside in her tight flight suit.

When she turns the corner and is out of sight, Nathan walks back into his stateroom, the door sliding closed behind him.

After turning off the lights and getting in bed, Nathan replays all the amazing sex they had tonight in his mind. He also mulls over the fact that he broke military regulations by fraternizing with a junior officer.

Before going to sleep he says to hell with regulations. What they have is too good to give up. If they are careful, they won't get caught.

CHAPTER 4 – THE TYRELLIAN SHIPYARDS

When Nathan wakes in his stateroom on the Invincible the next morning, he realizes this is not a dream. Less than twenty-four hours ago he officially took command of the battle carrier Invincible, and of the entire fleet when he was reinstated in the EDF.

As fleet admiral, he is one of the top ranked military officers on the planet, second only to the secretary of the fleet. As of a yet, a successor to the late Admiral Hollister has not been appointed. So, for now, Nathan is the top dog, answering directly to President Siebert.

Nathan's first twenty-four hours as fleet admiral could be described as "exciting" by anyone's standards. As Nathan gets out of bed, he wonders what excitement his second day in command will bring.

After finishing his morning routine, Nathan heads to his private dining room for breakfast, and then up to the bridge with a large black coffee.

After exiting the elevator, Nathan turns to his left and approaches the large doors that secure the command deck. As he approaches, the ship's computer scans and identifies him, grants him access, and opens the large steel and glass doors.

As he steps foot on the bridge, the ship's computer announces in its female voice, "Admiral on deck."

Everyone on the bridge immediately stands and snaps to attention.

The admiral walks over to the command chair and sits down.

"At ease everyone."

Everyone takes their station again.

"Chief of the Watch, status report."

"Aye sir, it was a quiet night and all systems are green. Nothing to report, sir."

The admiral says, "Thank you, Chief," then sits back in his seat and sips his coffee.

The XO walks over to Nathan's command chair and asks, "Orders, Admiral?"

"Well XO, since it's all quiet here, and the entire fleet is in orbit, why don't we take a little trip?"

"Aye sir. Where to, sir?"

"I understand that the Tyrellian shipyards have recently completed construction of our first, second-generation battle carrier, and that they have several more battle carriers and dreadnoughts in various stages of construction. I would like to visit the shipyards and see them for myself. I understand the shipyards are a technical marvel."

"Very well, sir. I wouldn't mind seeing them and the new battle carrier myself."

Nathan smiles and says, "Comms, send to all commands in battle group alpha. Form up on the Invincible, set course for the Tyrellian shipyards, and engage their FTL drives. Speed 14 TSL."

"Aye sir."

"Helm, set course for the Tyrellian shipyards."

"Aye sir, course plotted and laid in."

"Comms, has the battle group signaled they're ready?

"Aye sir."

"Excellent. Helm, engage the FTL drive, speed 14 TSL."

"Aye sir, engaging FTL drive now."

The battle group, comprised of about eighty ships, accelerates rapidly away from Earth, each ship disappearing in a bright blue flash of light.

A few minutes later Mr. Bell says, "Admiral, we have reached 14 TSL and will arrive at the Tyrellian shipyards in approximately seventy-four hours."

"Thank you, Helm."

Over the next three days, Nathan and the four officers he brought back to the EDF settle into life onboard a battle carrier.

Nathan also uses the time to test his crew, running several drills each day, pushing the crew to improve their response times. Throughout history, commanding officers have run drills to train their crew during times of peace, so they know exactly what to do in times of conflict and avoid panic. Advanced technology aside, the fact that they are in space, the most hostile environment ever, only emphasizes the need for drills. They must be prepared to face any situation they might encounter. There are many more dangers on a spaceship compared to an ocean-going ship. Worst-case scenarios being a major fire, loss of life support and or atmosphere. Nathan believes that practice makes perfect, so he has the crew run the drills again and again until he is happy with their response times.

At the end of each day, Nathan would head down to his private dining room for dinner and then retire to his state room for the evening. Around twenty-one hundred hours each night, Ms. Norata would surreptitiously make her way to Nathan's state room, dressed in a flight suit with some sexy lingerie on underneath. Nathan would let her in, and she would immediately strip off the flight suit and attack Nathan. After three to four hours of mind-blowing, crazy sex, Ms. Norata would slip the flight suit back on and carefully make her way back to her cabin.

Nathan cannot remember a time in his previous twenty-five years of military service where he slept so soundly. Even though he is only getting five or six hours of sleep at night, he is sleeping so deeply, that he is waking up totally refreshed and energized.

On the morning of the third day, Nathan wakes excited to see the shipyards and the new battle carrier with his own eyes.

After finishing his morning routine, Nathan heads to his private dining room for breakfast and then up to the bridge with a large black coffee.

After exiting the elevator, Nathan turns to his left and approaches the large doors that secure the command deck. As he approaches, the ship's computer scans and identifies him, grants him access and opens the large steel and glass doors.

As he steps foot on the bridge, the ship's computer announces in its female voice, "Admiral on deck."

Everyone on the bridge immediately stands and snaps to attention.

The admiral walks over to the command chair and sits down.

"At ease everyone."

Everyone takes their station again.

"Chief of the Watch, status report?"

"Aye sir, it was a quiet night and all systems are green. We are on course for the Tyrellian shipyards, traveling at 14 TSL. We should arrive in approximately two hours, sir."

The admiral says, "Excellent, thank you, Chief," then he sits back in his seat and sips his coffee.

A few minutes later Nathan says, "Comms, Admiral Jameson left before we did to oversee the finishing touches on the Vengeance. He should have arrived sometime yesterday. Can you see if you can contact him? I should probably let him know we'll be arriving in a couple of hours."

"Aye sir."

Five minutes go by and Nathan can hear his communications officer still trying to hail Admiral Jameson.

"Comms, any luck contacting Admiral Jameson?"

"No sir. I have tried all military frequencies with no response, from the admiral or from the Vengeance."

"That's odd."

"Yes sir, it's very odd."

"Well it's possible they are having issues with their comm system, after all it is a brand-new ship. Try hailing the Tyrellian shipyard and see what you can find out."

"Aye sir."

Five more minutes go by and Nathan can hear his communications officer still trying to hail the shipyard.

"Comms, any luck trying to raise the shipyard?"

"No sir. I'm not getting any response on any military or civilian frequencies."

Nathan looks at his XO standing beside him and says, "That is very odd. Something must be wrong."

"I would agree, Admiral."

"Comms, send to all commands, go to battle stations and inform them of what's going on.

"Aye sir."

"XO, sound battle stations."

"Aye sir.

The XO grabs the microphone and announces over the ship's address system, "Battle stations, battle stations, all hands man your battle stations, this is not a drill."

An alarm sounds after his address and the lights on the bridge change from white to red.

After a minute or so the XO says, "Admiral, all sections report battle stations manned and ready."

"Thank you, XO."

"CAG, the second we drop out of FTL, I want two squadrons of Tomcats in the air flying cover for the battle group."

"Aye sir."

"Comms, send to all commands in the battle group. If they see any Xandurian ships when we drop out of FTL, they are to open fire immediately. Don't wait for my order. Destroy all targets."

"Aye sir."

Nathan turns, looks at Ms. Norata and says, "Did you hear that Tactical? If you see a Xandurian ship after we drop out of FTL, open fire immediately. Don't wait for my order. Understood?"

"Understood, Admiral."

"Comms, keep trying to contact Admiral Jameson and the shipyard."

"Aye sir."

The next two hours go by very slowly. Nathan alternates between sitting on the edge of his command chair and pacing back and forth in front of it. To say he's anxious to get there would be an understatement.

The communications officer has not received a response to any of her hails. Nathan is expecting the worst.

After what seemed like an eternity a series of beeps comes from his console and then Mr. Bell says, "Admiral, one minute to the Tyrellian shipyards."

"Thank you, Helm."

"Tactical, anything on long range sensors?"

"Negative, Admiral. All I'm seeing is the main structure of the shipyard and what I'm guessing are our new ships being built."

"Very well, Tactical."

"Helm, drop us out of FTL."

"Aye sir, dropping us out of FTL now."

The crew sees a bright blue flash of light through the bridge windows and the Tyrellian shipyard instantly appears directly in front of the battle carrier. Or at least what's left of it. All the docks have been completely destroyed and the main structure has been shot to hell. There is no sign of anything resembling even a partially completed battle carrier or dreadnought, just a dozen very large debris fields. The shipyard was close to completing six new dreadnoughts and six new battle carriers, including the Vengeance, which had just started space trials. It appears as if all twelve ships have been destroyed.

Everyone on the bridge looks on in shock. They quickly snap out of it when a few F-114 Tomcats go screaming past the bridge at about five hundred knots as they head out on patrol.

"Tactical, scan the main structure for life signs and the surrounding area for escape pods, lifeboats and shuttles."

"Aye sir."

Nathan says, "Comms, get me President Siebert."

"Aye sir."

Ms. Norata says, "Admiral, there are no signs of life anywhere. No escape pods, lifeboats or shuttles. They made sure nobody survived."

"Thank you, Tactical."

The communications officer says, "Admiral, I have President Siebert for you, sir."

"On screen please, Comms."

"Aye sir."

President Siebert appears on screen sitting behind his desk, "Admiral Stone, I can tell by the look on your face you're not calling me with good news. What's happened?"

"Mr. President, the Tyrellian shipyard has been attacked. The shipyard and our new battle carriers and dreadnoughts have been destroyed. There are no survivors."

The look on the president's face changes to one of anger. He sits and says nothing for a few seconds and then says while gritting his teeth, "Do you know who it was?"

"I have no doubt that it was the Xandurians again, Mr. President. Who else could it be? We don't have a hostile relationship with anyone else at the moment."

"Can you get me some proof?"

"I believe I can, Mr. President. I'll send an engineering team over to what's left of the main structure and see if they can access the security recordings."

"If it was the Xandurians, what do you suggest we do about it?"

"Well Mr. President, I think the first thing I'm going to do is power up the time machine, jump back in time to an hour before the attack and blow those bastards to hell the second they drop out of FTL."

"Normally I would argue with you about the dangers of time travel, but I would hate to lose all those lives, the shipyards and our new ships. You have a green light, Admiral, good hunting."

"Thank you, Mr. President. Stone out."

Nathan presses a button on the command console on his chair to close the channel.

"Mr. Nagata, take an engineering team over to the main structure and get the computer system back online. Try to access the sensor logs and the security recordings. We need to find out the precise moment when the Xandurians arrive, and what their coordinates are when they drop out of FTL."

"Aye sir."

"Mr. Black, take a squad of Marines to protect Mr. Nagata and his team. You never know what's over there."

"Aye sir."

Mr. Nagata and Mr. Black get up from their stations, exit the bridge and head down to get their teams together for the mission.

"CAG, put another five full squadrons of Tomcats in the air, just in case the Xandurians try anything."

"Aye sir."

After putting on their space suits, the engineering team and the security team meet down in shuttle bay alpha, where they board a shuttle. Once everyone has taken their seats and have strapped in, the pilot closes the door, fires up the shuttle's systems and lifts off. He spins the shuttle ninety degrees and then nudges it towards the huge bay doors. Once the shuttle has passed through the shuttle bay's atmospheric force field and out into space, he rams the throttles wide open and turns the shuttle to head towards what is left of the shipyard's main structure.

It's a short flight from the battle carrier to the shuttle bays on the shipyard's main structure. As the shuttle approaches, the pilot turns on the shuttle's forward navigational flood lights, so he can see the structure.

The structure is heavily damaged, all power is down, and all the visible shuttle bay doors are closed. They have no easy way in.

The pilot takes the shuttle around the other side of main structure and finds a cargo bay with a large hole blown in the door. The hole looks large enough for the shuttle to fit through, but it will be a tight fit. The pilot slows the shuttle right down and lines it up with the hole in the bent and charred cargo bay door. He nudges the shuttle forward using only the RCS thrusters. The proximity alarm goes off when the shuttle gets within ten feet of the doors. The pilot makes several positional adjustments with the RCS thrusters as the ship passes through the hole in the door. He over corrects a little to port so the wingtip scrapes along the metal that is bent inwards from the hole. The scraping noise is very loud and high-pitched causing everyone in the shuttle to wince and cover their ears. The scraping also ratchets up the tension already felt by the engineers and the Marines. It takes the shuttle a little more than a minute to pass through the hole in the door and enter the cargo bay, but to the passengers it felt a lot longer.

The pilot sets the shuttle down gently on the floor of the cargo bay and engages the magnetic grappling system to hold the shuttle in place. Since the power inside the structure is off, there is no artificial gravity or life support.

Everyone in the shuttle puts on their space helmets and engages their magnetic boots before they depressurize the shuttle and open the door.

Mr. Black pulls up a holographic map of the structure and shows everyone where the main engineering section is and how to get there. Their first job is to get the power back on. Their second job is to get Nathan the information he needs.

Mr. Black sends half his Marines to sweep the corridors ahead to make sure the way is safe for the engineers. Mr. Nagata watches from the shuttle door as the Marines enter the dark corridor while turning on their helmet lights and the tactical lights mounted under the barrels of their pulse rifles. They move forward in pairs, walking hunched over and slightly crouched down, looking through the sights on their pulse rifles as they move. When they turn to look in a corner, they don't turn their heads, they turn their whole body and their pulse rifles. Their rifles point everywhere their eyes go. That way if they encounter something that could be hostile, their weapons are already pointed at it. The Marines check each room along the corridor to make sure it's clear before proceeding.

Once the first group of Marines has moved far enough ahead, the engineers and the rest of the Marines exit the shuttle. The

Marines surround the engineers and they all begin to walk towards the corridor. Again, the Marines are walking hunched over, looking through the sights of their pulse rifles. The two Marines at the back of the group turn around to “check their six” every twenty feet or so.

The journey from the cargo bay to the main engineering section is not a short one. The structure is very large and has many levels. They must go down ten levels from the cargo bay and then halfway across the main structure. The corridors are littered with debris and bodies. There are bundles of optic cable hanging everywhere from the ceiling. Whole sections of wall are blown apart and scorched black from power conduits exploding. The structure really took a pounding.

Everyone moves slowly in the dark corridors, checking every dark corner for possible threats and making sure they don’t trip on anything. In an environment like this, with tons of sharp edges jutting out from the damaged walls, and the debris scattered all over the floor, it would be very easy to puncture, cut or tear your space suit. Even a small cut in this situation could prove deadly.

They take about half an hour to reach the engineering section. When the first group of Marines arrives, they pry open the doors and secure the area. A few minutes later the engineers arrive with the second group or Marines. The engineers immediately get to work. They must get power to the main structure’s computer core so they can pull up the sensor logs and the security video footage Nathan has asked for.

Mr. Nagata quickly determines that the reactor is a lost cause. There is too much damage and too many blown out power conduits. There are two other redundant power systems left to investigate, the emergency power system and the batteries. Mr. Nagata assigns half of his team to each system to save time.

The first team and half of the Marines go to check the emergency power system in another section fifty meters down the corridor. When they get there, the Marines pry the doors open and everyone is stunned to see that almost the whole section is gone, completely destroyed, leaving what little was left exposed to space. The Marines force the doors closed again and then everyone heads back to the main engineering section.

The second team and the other half of the Marines take a short walk in the other direction to the section adjacent to main engineering where the batteries are located. The Marines pry the doors open and the team is surprised to find the batteries fully intact and full of power. Now to see if they can get this power to the computer core.

Mr. Nagata resets a few circuit breakers with no results. He and his team check the power conduits and soon discover they have been severed a few meters down the utility crawl space towards the main engineering section. Mr. Nagata decides to run a complete bypass and tasks his team and the Marines with gathering two hundred feet of undamaged power conduit so he can hook the batteries directly to the computer core. It takes the engineers and Marines almost three hours to find that much undamaged power conduit, cut it out and bring it back. It then takes the engineers another two hours to connect all the power conduit together and run it from the battery room, down the corridor, into main engineering, and hook it up to the power input terminals for the computer core.

All their hard work pays off when Mr. Nagata resets the circuits and the computer core powers up. The engineers and the Marines all high five each other on a job well done. Now they just have to hope that the computer core is undamaged, and they can retrieve the information Nathan needs for the time jump.

It takes a few minutes for the core to finish starting up, after which Mr. Nagata signs into the main terminal and checks to see if the core is undamaged. To his astonishment, he finds that the core is indeed intact and is able to access the sensor logs and the security video.

He scans back until he finds when the attacking ships drop out of FTL. He is not surprised at all to see the ships are Xandurian. Mr. Nagata downloads all the sensor logs and security videos from that moment until the computer core shut down to his tablet.

He then activates his suit's comm unit, "Nagata to Invincible, come in Invincible."

The Invincible's communication officer answers, "This is the Invincible, go ahead Commander Nagata."

"Put me through to Admiral Stone please."

"Yes, Commander Nagata, one moment."

A few seconds later Nathan comes on and says, "Mr. Nagata, do you have good news for me?"

"Yes, Admiral. We were able to power up the computer core and access the data you need. I have downloaded it to my tablet, and we are heading back to the shuttle. We should be back aboard the Invincible in about forty-five minutes."

"Excellent, good job, Mr. Nagata. Pass my thanks on to your team and to the Marines."

"Thank you, sir. I will, sir."

"See you shortly. Stone out."

The team begins its trip back to the cargo bay and the shuttle the same way it came in. Half the Marines go ahead to make sure the way is clear from danger, and the engineers and remaining Marines follow a few minutes later. Half an hour later the team makes it back to the cargo bay. Mr. Black, who had stayed in the shuttle to monitor the team, greets them at the open shuttle door.

"Great job, everyone. Now get on board and let's get the hell out of here."

When everyone is back onboard the shuttle, they close the door and replenish the atmosphere. Once everyone has taken their seats and strapped in, the pilot fires up the engines, releases the magnetic grappling system and lifts the ship off the deck using the RCS thrusters. He spins the shuttle around one hundred and eighty degrees and nudges it forward towards the hole in the shuttle bay doors once again. This time he manages to "thread the needle" perfectly, and the shuttle passes through the hole without touching the damaged cargo bay doors.

As soon as the shuttle is clear, he fires the main engines and heads towards the Invincible. It's a short flight, so soon the shuttle is entering shuttle bay alpha, through the port side bay doors, and setting down on the deck. The pilot shuts down the shuttle's systems and opens the door. Everyone exits the shuttle, and they head off, in different directions, across the shuttle bay.

After removing their space suits, Mr. Nagata and Mr. Black head back up to the bridge. Upon entering the bridge, Mr. Nagata walks over to Ms. Norata and hands her his tablet.

"Commander, here are the sensor logs and security videos from the moment just before the attacking ships drop out of FTL until the computer core shuts down."

"Thank you, Commander. I'll begin my analysis immediately."

Ms. Norata uploads all the data to the Invincible's main computer and begins her analysis. It doesn't take her long to pinpoint when the ships drop out of FTL, and what their exact coordinates and vectors were.

"Admiral, I have completed my analysis of the sensor logs and the security videos. I can now tell you exactly when and where the Xandurian ships drop out of FTL."

"Excellent, put the security videos on the main view screen please."

"Aye sir, playing them now."

The main view screen activates and shows four different video feeds. The videos show six large Xandurian warships drop out of FTL at exactly 09:33.42 the previous day. Almost exactly twenty-four hours before the Invincible and her battle group arrived this morning.

The Xandurian ships open fire immediately after dropping out of FTL. No warning at all. The shipyard was caught completely by surprise and didn't have time to raise its shields or activate its defenses. After blasting the hell out of the shipyard's main structure, the six Xandurian ships turn and start firing on the eleven unfinished ships and the recently completed battle carrier, Vengeance, which had just started space trials. The Vengeance didn't have a crew onboard yet so even though it was completed, there was no one onboard to raise the shields or to activate the weapons systems to shoot back.

It only took about ten minutes for the six Xandurian ships to destroy the twelve defenseless ships. After which they turned their weapons on the docks and obliterated them. When the Xandurians were finished, they turned one hundred and eighty degrees and jumped into FTL. A few seconds later, the shipyard's power fails, and the cameras shut down.

It is silent on the bridge except for the noises the ships systems make. Everyone is trying to process what they have just seen.

A few minutes later Nathan says, "Okay, everyone, now that we've witnessed the atrocity that took place here yesterday, what say we do something about it?"

Nathan looks around the bridge and each crew member nods their head in agreement.

"Excellent. CAG, get the fighters back onboard ASAP."

"Aye sir."

After about twenty minutes the CAG says, "All fighters are back on board, Admiral."

"Thank you, CAG."

"Mr. Nagata, head down to engineering and fire up the time machine."

Mr. Nagata says, "Aye sir," and then gets up, walks off the bridge, and heads to the elevators.

"Comms, send a message to the commanding officer of every ship in the battle group. Tell them to form up on the Invincible and that they must be well within a seven point five kilometer radius. It's going to get very crowded around here so tell them to use their thrusters and to move slowly and carefully so we don't have any collisions."

"Aye sir."

A few minutes later, ships start arriving and moving into close formation with the Invincible. There are two dreadnoughts in this battle group, and they pull up on either side the Invincible and begin to slowly side slip closer to the battle carrier.

Nathan walks up to the front bridge windows and watches nervously as these massive ships slip together as close as they can.

It's at that moment that the size of the dreadnoughts really sinks in. The Invincible and her sister ships are massive ships. They are a little over a mile and a half long, two-thirds of a mile wide and almost a third of a mile high from the bottom of the reactor domes to the top of the sensor mast. The dreadnoughts are almost twice the size of the Invincible, they are literally dwarfing what was once the largest ship in the galaxy. Having the massive dreadnoughts so close to the battle carrier is a bit... unsettling for Nathan.

Once the dreadnoughts are all tucked in tight, the escort carriers surround them and slip in as close as possible, followed by the battle cruisers, the light cruisers, and finally the destroyers.

When the last ship has maneuvered into place, it looks like a massive steel ball ten kilometers across floating in space. They have managed to tuck just about eighty war ships well inside the specified spherical diameter, so the fleet is now ready to jump back in time.

Nathan walks back over to his chair and pushes a button on the command console to activate the internal comm system.

"Mr. Nagata, is the time machine ready to go?"

"Yes Admiral, all systems are go for the time jump."

"Excellent. Thank you, Mr. Nagata."

Nathan pushes the button on his command console again to deactivate the internal comm system. He walks over to the control console for the time machine and powers it on. He checks to make sure that every part of every ship will be inside the bubble. The system gives him a green light indicating that every ship will be inside the bubble when it forms. Next, he sets the date and time to jump back to into the control console. Once he has set that, all that's left to do is press the execute button.

"Comms, give me an open channel to the battle group."

"Aye sir, channel open."

"Attention all commands, this is Admiral Stone. We are ready to execute the time jump. We are going to jump back in time a full two hours before the Xandurians arrive, so we have time to deploy the fleet and set our trap. Stand by for the count down."

Nathan pushes the execute button, the reactors' power output levels climb as the device forms the large time bubble around the battle group. The display on the control console shows a graphic of the bubble forming around the battle group and a power monitoring graph which is climbing quickly towards one hundred percent.

When the graph reaches ninety-five percent Nathan says, "Time jump in 5... 4... 3... 2... 1... now."

The graph hits one hundred percent, there is a momentary flash of bright white light and then the power levels drop quickly to zero as the bubble collapses.

A few seconds later the communications officer says, "Admiral Stone, we are being hailed by the Tyrellians."

"Thank you, Comms, on speakers please."

"Aye sir, on speakers."

Over the speakers the bridge crew hears, "Attention EDF fleet commander, this is Yard Master Zyalla, come in please."

"Yard Master Zyalla, this is Admiral Nathan Stone on the Invincible."

"Admiral Stone, would you mind explaining your sudden appearance and the purpose of your visit? You weren't scheduled to arrive until tomorrow."

"My apologies for our unannounced and sudden appearance Yard Master, there was no way to inform you of our early arrival."

"What do you mean there was no way to inform me of your early arrival? You have a working comm system, don't you?"

"Yes, of course, Yard Master, but radio signals can't travel back in time."

"I beg your pardon, Admiral?"

"We traveled back in time approximately twenty-nine hours Yard Master. We came from the future."

"That's not possible. Time travel is not possible."

"Oh, I assure you, Yard Master, it's quite possible."

"That's unbelievable, Admiral Stone."

"I'm telling you the truth, sir."

"Okay, let's assume for a moment that I believe you. Why did you travel back in time to get here a day early?"

"Well, sir, this is going to be kind of hard to hear."

"I'm listening."

"Well, sir, when we arrived at your shipyards and dropped out of FTL, we discovered that your shipyard had been attacked and completely destroyed along with the battle carriers and dreadnoughts that you are currently building for us."

"Seriously, Admiral Stone, you expect me to believe all of this?"

"I have proof of everything I'm telling you, Yard Master."

"Very well, show me your proof."

"Comms, transmit the security video and sensor logs over to the Yard Master."

"Aye sir, transmitting now."

"Yard Master, we are sending you the security video and sensor logs we recovered from your own systems after we arrived and found your shipyards destroyed. The videos show six large Xandurian warships drop out of FTL and attack without warning. They badly damage your main complex, destroy your docks and our ships. They leave no survivors. After determining when the Xandurians arrive, we jumped back in time to stop them from destroying your shipyards."

"Very well, Admiral Stone, I will examine your evidence and get back to you. Zyalla out."

Mr. Black says, "He doesn't sound too grateful, does he?"

"Well, that is a lot to take in, Mr. Black."

"I suppose it is, sir."

"In the meantime, let's get the fleet into position, shall we?"

"Comms, send a message to the commanding officers of every ship in the battle group. Tell them to disperse and deploy, standard fleet formation."

"Aye sir."

The communications officer sends the message. Soon ships on the outer edge of the ball begin to peel off and spread out. It takes about half an hour for all the ships in the fleet to disperse. The last ones to separate are the dreadnoughts as they were at the center of the ball of ships with the Invincible. Nathan and the bridge crew watch as the dreadnoughts roll slightly and begin to turn and pull away from the Invincible. It's impressive to see these huge battleships maneuver from this close.

After a minute or two more, the communications officer says, "Admiral, all commands report they have dispersed and are getting into standard fleet formation."

"Thank you, Comms."

After the dreadnoughts move away from the Invincible, the bridge crew can now see the undamaged Tyrellian shipyards. The shipyards are a buzzing beehive of activity, with all manner of small work pods, tugs and shuttles flying in every direction. They also see the six new dreadnoughts and the five new battle carriers under construction in the massive automated docks. Through the open ends of the docks they see massive mechanical arms putting large hull plates in place and welding them to the inner structures with laser welders. Just to the right of the main structure the bridge crew sees the recently completed battle carrier, Vengeance, moored to a dock with several gangways attached to it.

Nathan stands up and walks over to the front bridge windows, taking it all in, "Now that is impressive."

After taking in the sights for a minute, Nathan turns to Mr. Bell and says, "Helm, bring up a chart and pull up the sensor data from the shipyards. I want you to show me, the position of the shipyards, the current position of our battle group and the coordinates for the Xandurian ships the second they drop out of FTL."

"Aye sir."

Nathan walks over to Mr. Bell's station, leans on his chair and looks over his shoulder at his display. Mr. Bell pulls all the requested information together and brings it up on his display.

Nathan puts his finger on Mr. Bell's display about halfway between the shipyard and the coordinates where the Xandurian ships will drop out of FTL.

"I want you to put us right about here, approximately five kilometers in front of the Xandurians."

"Aye sir."

Mr. Bell plots the course and moves the Invincible into position.

When he has brought the ship to a full stop, Mr. Bell says, "We're in position, Admiral, holding station exactly five kilometers from the specified coordinates."

"Thank you, Helm."

"Comms, send a message to the commanding officers of every ship in the battle group. Tell them to deploy their ships in a standard thirty-degree arc formation on either side of us."

"Aye sir."

"We're going to set up an old-style shooting gallery. The second they drop out of FTL we're going to hit them with everything we've got. They're in for a real surprise."

Nathan turns to look at Ms. Norata and he can tell she's a little excited, "Tactical, calculate both the flight time of our ship to ship missiles and of the laser cannon blasts to the coordinates where the Xandurians will drop out of FTL. I want our weapons contacting their ships the second they drop out of FTL."

"Aye sir."

"Once you have those calculations, I want you to coordinate the attack with the rest of the fleet's tactical officers."

"Aye sir."

Nathan looks up at the clock above the main view screen. It is showing 08:03:27. An hour and a half before the Xandurians arrive.

Nathan says, "Comms, send a message to all commands in the battle group, have them go to battle stations."

"Aye sir."

"XO, sound battle stations."

"Aye sir."

The XO grabs the microphone and announces over the ship's address system, "Battle stations, battle stations, all hands man your battle stations, this is not a drill."

An alarm sounds after his address and the lights on the bridge change from white to red.

After a minute or so the XO says, "Admiral, all sections report battle stations manned and ready."

"Thank you, XO."

"Comms, send a message to all commands in the battle group, have them direct their laser cannon turrets at the coordinates where the Xandurian ships will drop out of FTL and deploy their ship to ship missile launchers."

"Aye sir."

"Tactical, direct our laser cannon turrets at the coordinates where the Xandurian ships will drop out of FTL and deploy the ship to ship missile launchers."

"Aye sir."

At dozens of locations all over the battle carrier, missile bay doors open, missile launchers rise and spin to face straight forward.

"Comms, send a message to all commands in the battle group, tell them to engage their cloaking devices."

"Aye sir."

"Tactical, engage the cloaking device."

"Aye sir, engaging the cloaking device now."

One by one all the ships in the battle group fade out and disappear as their cloaking devices engage.

"Tactical, what's the calculated flight time for our ship to ship missiles?"

"Thirty-five seconds from the time I press the fire button until the missiles contact their hulls, sir."

"And you've sent these numbers to the rest of the battle group?"

"Yes sir."

"Excellent, thank you, Tactical."

Nathan sits back in his chair and thinks to himself, "The fleet is ready, now we sit and wait."

CHAPTER 5 – THE MASSACRE

The next hour and a half goes by very slowly on the bridge of the Invincible. It's quiet on the bridge save for the usual beeps and noises from the computer systems. The crew isn't talking very much, and Nathan isn't giving any orders. He is simply sitting back in his chair, his hands clasped in front of his face, fingers interlocked, elbows resting on the arms of his chair, staring at the main viewscreen and the clock above it.

When the clock finally displays 09:30.00, Nathan stands up and walks over to the tactical station where Ms. Norata is double checking the coordinates and the status of the weapons and defensive systems. Nathan knows she is the best tactical officer in the fleet, so he refrains from asking her if everything is correct and ready. He knows she has already triple checked everything in the last five minutes.

When the clock displays 09:31:00 Nathan turns towards the communications officer and says, "Comms, open a channel to the battle group and leave it open until after the battle is over."

"Aye sir, channel open."

"Attention all tactical officers. Arm your ship to ship missiles and prepare to fire on my command."

Ms. Norata arms the Invincible's ship to ship missiles and scans for ships approaching in FTL.

"Admiral, my scanners are showing six ships approaching our position in FTL."

"Thank you, Tactical."

Nathan watches the clock until it says 09:33:00 and says, "Attention all tactical officers. Fire missiles in 5... 4... 3... 2... 1... fire, fire, fire."

Ms. Norata presses the button to launch the ship to ship missiles. Each launcher can fire a dozen missiles at a time. There are dozens of launchers aimed at the coordinates, so she just launched hundreds of missiles from the Invincible. There are roughly eighty ships in the battle group. Some have more missile launchers than others. All totaled the battle group just launched over ten thousand missiles at the six incoming Xandurian ships.

Nathan and the rest of the bridge crew anxiously watch the next thirty seconds tick away.

Nathan says, "Here they come, in 3... 2... 1... now."

The six Xandurian ships drop out of FTL at exactly 09:33:42 at the same coordinates gathered from the shipyard's sensor logs. One second after the Xandurian ships drop out of FTL, the missiles slam into their shields. The explosions from the ten thousand plus missiles are an impressive sight to behold, but they obscure the six Xandurian ships behind a curtain of fire for about thirty seconds. When the fireball clears, Nathan and his bridge crew can see that the lead ship at the center of the group was pushed sideways into the flight path of the ship next to it, causing a collision between the two large warships.

Each ship sustained massive amounts of damage and they are out of commission. The ships are fused together and are in a slow, uncontrolled spin, drifting to the starboard side from the Earth ships' point of view. The other four Xandurian ships have sustained quite a bit of damage but are still maneuverable and under way.

Upon seeing this, Nathan says, "Attention all tactical officers, reload your missile launchers, bring all possible laser cannon turrets to bear and open fire. Fire at will."

A few seconds later, all eighty EDF warships open up with their huge laser cannons, each volley sending several thousand red laser blasts hurtling towards the six Xandurian ships.

It's safe to say at this point the six Xandurian ships are doomed. The first wave of ship to ship missiles caused massive amounts of damage. Their shields are down to a mere ten percent and won't last long under the intense barrage from the Earth ships. It takes less than a minute for the Xandurians' shields to drop, and then the blasts from the Earth ships' laser cannons begin to chew away at their hulls.

It only takes another couple of minutes before the Xandurian ships begin to explode. The first to go are the two ships fused together by the collision. They both disappear in a massive explosion and fireball. One by one the other four soon follow suit.

When the last ship explodes, the bridge crew on the Invincible jump up out of their chairs and cheer. Nathan's plan has worked perfectly. By jumping back in time, they were able to launch a preemptive strike and destroy the Xandurian ships before they could fire a single shot. They saved the Tyrellian shipyards, Earth's twelve new ships and the lives of all beings present.

Nathan walks back to his chair and says, "Attention all commands. Well done everyone. Disengage your cloaking devices and stand down from battle stations. Stone out," then he pushes a button on the command console on his chair to close the channel.

"Tactical, disengage the cloaking device."

"Aye sir, disengaging the cloaking device now."

"XO, stand down from battle stations."

"Aye sir.

The XO grabs the microphone and announces over the ship's address system, "Attention all hands, stand down from battle stations, repeat stand down from battle stations."

A chime sounds after his address and the lights on the bridge change from red to white.

One by one all the ships in the battle group begin to appear as their cloaking devices disengage.

Nathan doesn't want to spend any more time in the past than he has to, so he decides to get the fleet moving.

"Comms, send a message to the commanding officer of every ship in the battle group. Tell them to form up on the Invincible again and remind them to use their thrusters and to move slowly and carefully so we don't have any collisions."

"Aye sir."

A few minutes later, ships start arriving and moving into close formation with the Invincible. Once again, the two dreadnoughts pull up on either side of the Invincible and begin to slowly side slip closer to the battle carrier. Once the dreadnoughts are all tucked in tight, the escort carriers surround them and slip in as close as possible followed by the battle cruisers, the light cruisers, and finally the destroyers.

When the last ship has maneuvered into place and they once again have what looks like a massive steel ball ten kilometers across floating in space, Nathan pushes a button on the command console on his chair to activate the internal comm system.

"Mr. Nagata is the time machine ready to go?"

"Yes Admiral, all systems are go for the time jump."

"Excellent, thank you, Mr. Nagata."

Nathan pushes the button on his command console again to deactivate the internal comm system.

He walks over to the control console for the time machine and powers it on. He checks to make sure that every part of every ship will be inside the bubble. The system gives him a green light indicating that every ship will be inside the bubble when it forms. Next, Nathan goes to set the date and time to jump forward to into the control console. Nathan wants to jump ahead to one minute after the fleet jumped back in time. Once he has set that, all that's left to do is press the execute button.

"Comms, open a channel to the battle group."

"Aye sir, channel open."

"Attention all commands, this is Admiral Stone. We are ready to execute the time jump. We're going to jump ahead to one minute after we jumped back in time. Stand by for the count down."

Nathan pushes the execute button, the reactors' power output levels climb as the device forms the large time bubble around the battle group. The display on the control console shows a graphic of the bubble forming around the battle group as well as a power monitoring graph which is climbing quickly towards one hundred percent.

When the graph reaches ninety-five percent Nathan says, "Time jump in 5... 4... 3... 2... 1... jump."

The graph hits one hundred percent, there is a momentary flash of bright white light, and then the power levels drop quickly to zero as the bubble collapses. Nathan powers off the time machine control console.

"Attention all commands, jump complete. We are back where we started from. Stone out."

He walks back over to his chair and pushes a button on the command console on his chair to close the channel.

A few seconds later the communications officer says, "Admiral Stone, we are being hailed by Yard Master Zyalla."

"Thank you, Comms, on speakers please."

"Aye sir, on speakers."

Over the speakers, the bridge crew hears, "Attention, Admiral Stone, this is Yard Master Zyalla, come in please."

"Yard Master Zyalla, this is Admiral Stone on the Invincible."

"Ah yes, Admiral, I'm glad to see you made it back. I have to say, watching your fleet disappear in the blink of an eye yesterday and then watching you reappear just as abruptly today is very fascinating. What do you experience during the jump?"

"Yes, I'm sure it is, Yard Master. Actually, we just see a bright white flash of light and that's it."

"Nothing else?"

"Nope, just the flash of light. The trip through time is instantaneous to us."

"Again, fascinating. Now, Admiral, back to why you made the journey out to my shipyards. I'm guessing as the newly appointed fleet admiral you wanted to see how your new ships are being built?"

"You are correct, Yard Master Zyalla."

"Well, Admiral Stone, a tour of the facility is the least I can do to thank you for saving all of our lives. I will await your arrival in shuttle bay one."

"Excellent, I will see you shortly. Stone out."

"Comms, send a message to the commanding officers of every ship in the battle group. Tell them to disperse and deploy, standard fleet formation."

"Aye sir."

The communications officer sends the message and soon ships on the outer edge of the ball begin to peel off and spread out. It takes about half an hour for all the ships in the fleet to disperse. The last ones to separate are the dreadnoughts as they were at the center of the ball of ships with the Invincible. Nathan and the bridge crew watch as the dreadnoughts roll slightly and begin to turn and pull away from the Invincible.

After a minute or two more, the communications officer says, "Admiral, all commands report they have dispersed and are getting into standard fleet formation."

"Thank you, Comms."

After the dreadnoughts move away from the Invincible, the bridge crew can once again see the undamaged Tyrellian shipyards.

The shipyards are still a buzzing beehive of activity with all manner of small work pods, tugs and shuttles flying in every direction, working away like nothing ever happened. The six new dreadnoughts and the five new battle carriers are still being worked on in the massive automated docks and the Vengeance is still moored to the dock with several gangways attached to it.

To see what, just a few hours ago, was a scene of mass destruction, brought back to life like nothing ever happened, is amazing to say the least. They have quite literally turned back the hands of time.

CHAPTER 6 – WAS IT A TRAP?

Nathan turns and heads towards the large glass and steel doors at the back of the bridge and says, "XO you have the con. I'm taking a shuttle over to the shipyards for my tour."

"Aye sir."

Nathan pauses, turns back and says, Ms. Norata, Mr. Black, Mr. Bell, you're with me.

All three crew members reply, "Aye sir."

They get up out of their chairs and turn to walk towards Nathan at the back of the bridge. Other crew members that were manning secondary systems take over their stations.

"Comms, have Mr. Nagata meet us in shuttle bay alpha. I think he will enjoy this tour more than any of us."

"Aye sir."

Nathan and his three crew members exit the bridge through the large glass and steel doors, which open as they approach, and take an elevator down to the carrier's internal tram. There is a tram sitting there waiting when they exit the elevator, so they take it to shuttle bay alpha. After arriving at the shuttle bay, Nathan and his three crew members step off the tram and walk over to one of the shuttles. As they approach, they see Mr. Nagata walking across the shuttle bay towards them.

All five of them board the shuttle, take their seats and strap in. Mr. Bell takes the pilot's seat, closes the door, fires up the shuttle's systems and lifts off. He spins the shuttle ninety degrees and then nudges it towards the huge bay doors. Once the shuttle has passed through the shuttle bay's atmospheric force field and out into space, Mr. Bell plots a course around the other ships escorting the battle carrier and pushes the throttles halfway open.

Mr. Nagata says, "Thank you for inviting me along, Admiral. I can't wait to see these shipyards in action."

"Of course, Mr. Nagata, out of the five of us I think you will get the most out of this tour."

"Absolutely, sir."

Once clear of the fleet, Mr. Bell flies straight at the shipyard's main structure. As they get closer, he lines the shuttle up with shuttle bay one and pulls back on the throttles. He slows the shuttle down to a crawl, takes it through the atmospheric force field and sets it down on the deck of the shuttle bay. Mr. Bell shuts the shuttle's systems down, opens the door, and then the five of them exit the shuttle. As Nathan steps down onto the deck, Yard Master Zayalla walks into the bay.

The Tyrellians are very much like humans, save for a few minor differences. They have wide, flat noses that mold right into their cheeks, their skin is a medium red color, they all have white hair on top of their heads and the colored parts of their eyes, what we call the iris, are shiny silver.

He extends his right hand to shake Nathan's and says, "It's a pleasure to meet you, Admiral Stone, and welcome to my shipyard."

Nathan says, "It's a pleasure to meet you as well, Yard Master Zayalla. Allow me to introduce my tactical officer, Commander Norata, my helmsman, Commander Bell, my Marine guard captain, Lieutenant Colonel Black and my chief engineer, Lieutenant Commander Nagata."

"It is a pleasure to meet you all, and welcome to my shipyard. Now if you will all follow me, we will begin the tour in the main control room."

The yard master leads them out of the shuttle bay and down a long corridor to a set of elevators. After boarding the elevator, the yard master presses the button at the top of the control panel. The elevator rises quickly and soon arrives at the very top of the shipyard's main structure. When the elevator doors open, they step out into the most high-tech control center that any of them have ever seen.

The shipyards are touted as being fully automated, so each dock has its own control station complete with a large holographic display and a large curved wall of video displays. The holographic displays give the dock supervisors a full three-hundred-and-sixty-degree, 3D representation of the dock that they can walk around and interact with. It displays the dock, the ship that is being built, the mechanical arms, and all the small work craft that deliver parts and maneuver them into position. The large curved walls of video displays provide the dock supervisors with all kinds of information like detailed views of the parts supply lines, close-up views of what each mechanical arm is doing, a detailed task list that shows him what is left to do on the ship in his dock, and a work craft status display.

Each dock is controlled by its own separate computer system and each dock is monitored by a dock supervisor. There are no people out in space working on building the ships in the docks. The shipyards work around the clock with speed and precision due to their level of automation.

There are twenty-four docks in the shipyard so there are also twenty-four control stations in the control center. The control center is a large, round section, whose exterior walls, and much of the ceiling, are made from thick glass panels so the dock supervisors can also look out the windows to see what is going on in their docks.

To say that Nathan and his officers are impressed would be an understatement. Never have they seen such an impressive automated manufacturing system.

Yard Master Zayalla takes some time to show them how everything works at one of the control stations and then walks them over to the glass wall so they can see the docks directly.

Nathan looks down on the dock right in front of him where a new dreadnought is nearing completion, and he marvels at its size.

Beyond that he sees his battle group sitting in space about ten kilometers away. He can clearly make out the Invincible and the two dreadnoughts from here.

Suddenly, there is a flash of bright white light. The Invincible and three other ships to its starboard side, including one of the dreadnoughts, shatter into millions of small pieces. The pieces are strewn in tight, defined trails, on a downward angle, for several kilometers to their port sides.

Less than a second later, massive explosions engulf the areas where the ships used to be.

Nathan's eyes well up with tears, he feels sick to his stomach, every muscle in his body tenses up to the point of tearing, he slams his fists on the glass and yells, "NO, NO, NO, NO, NOOOOOOOOOOOO", and then hangs his head.

Ms. Norata starts to shake, her stomach ties itself in knots and she yells, "OH MY GOD, NO, NO, NO," puts her right hand on Nathan's shoulder, brings her left hand up to cover her mouth, and sobs uncontrollably.

Mr. Nagata's face goes bright red and his heart rate skyrockets. With massive amounts of adrenaline being pumped into his system he yells, "FUUUUCK", and kicks a nearby chair, sending it flying about fifteen feet, crashing into a wall.

Mr. Black points at the explosions with his right index finger and looks at his team members on his right and on his left while backing up. Random words are coming out of his mouth, but he is talking so softly that no one can hear what he is saying. He is not watching where he is stepping as he is backing up and he trips over a power cord, falling backwards, his butt hitting the floor, his back landing against one of the control stations. He covers his face with both hands to hide the tears that are rolling down his cheeks.

Mr. Bell doesn't move, doesn't say a word. He doesn't react at all. He just stands there staring blankly at where four ships, including the Invincible, used to be.

When the explosions clear, all that is left are small chunks of debris, which have been sent hurtling in all directions.

Nathan and his team have just witnessed the instantaneous deaths of over forty-eight thousand people, the crew complement of the four ships.

Trying his best to contain his anger, Nathan turns and looks at Yard Master Zayalla and asks through clenched teeth, pointing out the window, "Do you have any idea what kind of weapon could have done that?"

More than a little flustered, the yard master backs up a few steps and says, "No Admiral, I do not know of any weapons capable of destroying ships in this manner. This must be something new."

Nathan nods his head slightly and then says, "We better get back to the battle group."

"Of course, Admiral, I will escort you down to the shuttle bay."

Ms. Norata takes Mr. Bell by the arm and Nathan helps Mr. Black to his feet. The six of them head over to the elevators and take one back down to the level containing shuttle bay one. The yard master leads them back down the long corridor, into the shuttle bay, and back over to their shuttle.

When they get to the shuttle, the yard master turns and says, "I would like to offer my deepest condolences on the loss of your ships and their crews. If there is anything we can do, please let me know."

Nathan and his officers all nod to say thank you to Yard Master Zayalla for his kind words and then they board the shuttle and take their seats.

Before they close the door, the yard master says, "Safe journey my friends," and then turns and walks away.

Mr. Bell fires up the shuttle's systems and lifts off. He spins the shuttle around one hundred and eighty degrees and then nudges it out into space. Once the shuttle has passed through the shuttle bay's atmospheric force field, he rams the throttles wide open. He wants to get Nathan back to the fleet as soon as possible.

Nathan activates the shuttle's comm system and says, "Attention EDF dreadnought, this is Fleet Admiral Nathan Stone, come in please."

A few seconds later he receives a response, "Admiral Stone, this is Admiral Anderson on the Aurora."

"Glad you're still with us, Admiral Anderson. My party and I are just leaving the shipyard's main structure in a shuttle. I'm transferring my flag to the Aurora. We'll be onboard in two minutes. As soon as we land, I want the fleet underway, headed for home at maximum speed. Understood?"

"Understood, Admiral Stone. Tell your pilot he's cleared for landing in landing bay alpha, port side. Oh, and Admiral, I'm glad you're still with us as well."

"Thank you, Admiral Anderson. I'll see you on the bridge shortly. Stone out."

Nathan shuts down the comm system and says, "You heard him, Mr. Bell."

"Aye sir."

As they approach the port side of the dreadnought, Mr. Bell lines the shuttle up with the huge entrance to landing bay alpha. As he gets closer, he slows the shuttle down to almost a slow crawl. Soon the shuttle is passing through the atmospheric force field and into the landing bay. Once fully inside, Mr. Bell sets the shuttle down on the deck. He quickly shuts down the shuttle's systems, opens the door and they all step out into the Aurora's massive landing bay.

Nathan turns and looks out through the huge landing bay doors as the dreadnought, and the rest of the battle group, accelerate rapidly away from the shipyards. He sees a bright blue flash of light followed by stars streaking past the open bay doors.

Nathan turns back to see a familiar face, Lieutenant Green, coming towards them. When he reaches Nathan, he stops, snaps to attention, and salutes him.

"Admiral Stone, welcome aboard the Aurora, sir. It is nice to see you again, though I wish it was under better circumstances."

Nathan returns his salute and says, "Thank you, Lieutenant Green, it's nice to see you again as well."

"Admiral Anderson sent me to escort you and your party to the bridge, sir."

"Very well, Lieutenant, lead on."

Lieutenant Green, Nathan and his party head off across the huge, busy landing bay. Lieutenant Green leads them over to the internal tram and they take it to the center of the huge dreadnought. After that they take an elevator up to the bridge. When the elevator stops and the doors open, everyone steps out, Nathan being the last to leave the elevator.

As Nathan steps foot on the bridge, the ship's computer announces in its female voice, "Admiral on deck."

Everyone on the bridge immediately stands and snaps to attention.

"At ease everyone."

Everyone takes their station again.

Admiral Anderson walks over and extends his hand to shake Nathan's, "Admiral Stone, welcome aboard the Aurora, it's nice to see you again, sir, though I wish it was under better circumstances."

Nathan shakes Admiral Anderson's hand and says, "Thank you Admiral Anderson, it's nice to see you again as well."

"I'm very sorry about the Invincible, Admiral Stone. I know she was special to you."

"As were the people aboard her, Admiral Anderson. It's hard losing a command, but it's even harder dealing with the deaths of thousands. Let us not forget we lost four ships and well over forty-eight-thousand lives today."

"Yes, of course, Admiral."

Nathan says, "Admiral, since we don't know anything about the weapon that destroyed our ships, I want you to cloak the fleet until we get back to Earth."

"Aye sir."

Admiral Anderson turns and walks to his station at the center of the bridge and says, "Comms, open a channel to the battle group."

"Aye sir, channel open."

"Attention all commands, this is Admiral Anderson on the Aurora. Engage your cloaking devices. Anderson out."

The admiral presses a button on the command console on his chair to close the channel.

"Tactical, engage the cloaking device."

"Aye sir, engaging cloaking device now."

Everyone on the bridge watches through the port and starboard side bridge windows as the other ships in the battle group fade out and disappear.

Nathan adds, "Admiral, we don't know if the rest of the fleet back at Earth is being targeted, so have your communications officer dispatch a message. Have the fleet spread out into high orbit and engage their cloaking devices. In the meantime, let's examine any available sensor data and video feeds to see if we can figure out what the hell happened."

"Aye sir."

Admiral Anderson walks over to his communications officer and instructs her to send the message to the fleet back home in orbit around Earth. He then goes over to his tactical officer and instructs her to collect the video feeds and sensor logs from any ships close to the Invincible and the other destroyed ships at the time of the attack. It takes about half an hour for the Aurora's tactical officer to gather the video feeds and sensor logs from the other ships in the battle group.

When he has gathered all the requested data, the Aurora's tactical officer says, "Admiral Anderson, I have the data you requested. Where would you like to examine it, sir?"

"Thank you, Tactical. Upload it to the computer in the holographic battle control center and then have the computer generate a holographic simulation."

"Aye sir, uploading the data now. The simulation should be ready in just a few moments."

Nathan looks at Admiral Anderson and asks, "Holographic battle control center?"

"Yes Admiral, it allows us to generate a live 3D holographic display of a battle both for tactical and training purposes. Here let me show you."

Admiral Anderson motions with his right hand towards a door that is behind and to the right of the tactical station. The admiral leads Nathan and his party over to door and places his right hand on a biometric hand scanner. A thick white line of light scans from the tips of his fingers to the heel of his palm. The scanner turns green and displays a message that says, "Access Granted Admiral Anderson." The solid white metal door slides open to reveal a large dimly lit room with a large round control center in the middle of the floor with a large conical display panel suspended from the ceiling.

"Come in everyone, the simulation should be ready in just a minute."

After the six of them enter the room, the lights come on, the displays and the control center power up, and the door slides closed behind them. The room has the same high-tech appearance as the bridge, adorned in white with black and blue display panels and bright blue accent lights.

Just then the tactical officer's voice comes over the speakers, "The simulation is ready, Admiral. The file name is Invincible DIA 01 Alpha."

"Thank you, Tactical."

"Computer, display simulation, Invincible DIA 01 Alpha."

"Aye sir, displaying Invincible DIA 01 Alpha now."

The top of the round control center lights up bright white and then a perfect 3D display of the battle group appears about two feet above it.

Nathan says, "Very impressive, Admiral, I can see how this would be useful in a battle."

"Oh yes, Admiral, but you haven't seen anything yet."

"Computer, isolate and zoom in on the four ships that were destroyed."

"Aye sir, zooming in."

The computer zooms in until only the four ships that were destroyed are displayed. Nathan notices how detailed the 3D projections of the ships are and he is very impressed.

"Computer, fast forward to one second before the ships explode and then play at one tenth of normal speed."

"Aye sir, playing simulation at one tenth speed."

The simulation plays, but one tenth speed turns out to be too fast. The debris trails just suddenly appear, and the ships are torn apart without showing them what did the damage.

"Computer, reset and play at one twentieth of normal speed."

"Aye sir, playing simulation at one twentieth speed."

The computer starts the simulation again, but even at one twentieth speed, whatever has caused the damage is moving too fast.

Looking up at Nathan, Admiral Anderson says, "Maybe the third time's a charm. Computer, reset and play at one one hundredth of normal speed."

"Aye sir, playing simulation at one one hundredth speed."

The computer starts the simulation again, but even at one one hundredth speed, whatever has caused the damage is moving too fast.

With a little frustration in his voice, Nathan says, "I think we're going about this all wrong, Admiral. May I?"

"Of course, Admiral, be my guest."

"Computer, analyze the video feeds and sensor data. If you slow the simulation down exponentially, do the objects that cause the damage become visible at some point?"

"I will run the analysis. One moment please."

Not normally an impatient man, Nathan paces back and forth beside the control center with his arms crossed over his chest, anxious for the results.

After a few minutes the computer says, "Analysis complete. The objects appear when playback was slowed..."

Nathan cuts the computer off and says in a raised voice, "Display the objects when they first appear and indicate their trajectory using a thin, red, dotted line."

"Aye sir."

At the edge of the display, angled down at the ships, appear four black and green missile-like projectiles. The computer adds the thin, red, dotted lines showing their trajectory. The thin, red, dotted lines appear to be on about a forty-five-degree downward angle. One dotted line passes through the middle of the light cruiser, another through the middle of the heavy cruiser. Everyone in the room immediately takes note that all four dotted lines pass through the dreadnought and the Invincible.

Nathan moves around the table and examines the simulation from all angles. Many questions are running through his mind. He needs to see more.

"Computer, very slowly, advance the video and show us the projectiles passing through the ships and the damage they cause."

"Aye sir."

The projectiles begin traveling down the dotted lines towards the four ships. As the projectiles contact the hulls of the two cruisers, everyone is amazed at the amount of damage they inflict on the ships. Compared to the size of the ships, these projectiles are small, but as they pass through the hulls, they release enough energy to completely shatter the center of both cruisers into millions of small pieces. Crashing through the cruisers, doesn't slow them down or even alter their path in the slightest. All four projectiles continue on, cutting through the dreadnought, and finally through the Invincible. The projectiles shatter the hulls of the two huge ships in their entirety.

Trails of debris follow down the dotted lines as the projectiles travel down and away from the ships. The projectiles tore through four ships like they weren't even there. What kind of technology could do that?

As the projectiles reach the edge of the control center, the computer pauses the simulation. Everyone present is speechless as they gaze upon the simulation. Two cruisers and two of the largest ships in the galaxy utterly decimated, without the use of any explosive.

Nathan is the first to react asking, "Computer, can you calculate how fast the projectiles are moving as they impact the first ships?"

"Aye sir. I calculate that the projectiles are moving at approximately 12.25 TSL."

Nathan turns and looks at Admiral Anderson and says, "That explains it."

"Yes, it does, and we have a big problem."

"Yes, we certainly do."

Mr. Nagata says, "Son of a bitch."

Ms. Norata asks, "Someone developed a weapon that travels faster than the speed of light?"

Nathan responds, "It appears so."

Mr. Black blurts out, "Holy shit."

Nathan says, "Holy shit indeed. The energy these things release on impact is unimaginable. Now that we know what we're dealing with, we better inform the president and warn the rest of the fleet."

Admiral Anderson heads towards the door, "I'm on it, Admiral," and then re-enters the bridge.

Ms. Norata asks, "Admiral, do you think the Xandurians specifically targeted the Invincible? Lured us here by destroying the shipyards? Got us to show our hand?"

"I was thinking the same thing, Ms. Norata. They set up a scenario where they knew I wouldn't be able to resist using the time machine to stop them from destroying the shipyards, there by confirming the time machine was onboard the Invincible."

Mr. Bell asks, "Why would they do that?"

"Well, we destroyed the time machine they were building, then we destroyed Trynx 3, the only known source of the time ore needed to power a time machine, so building themselves another one became pointless. After that we stopped them from stealing our working time machine and the remaining ore and brought it onboard the Invincible to keep it safe, or so we thought. With the time machine installed in the Invincible's engineering area, the Xandurians must have figured they had no chance of getting their hands on it, so I'm guessing they decided that if they can't have it, then nobody can."

Mr. Black says, "I guess that makes sense. Hell of a plan."

Nathan leans down and puts his elbows on the control center and shakes his head, "Indeed, Mr. Black, and I fell for it. I didn't see it coming at all."

"Don't be too hard on yourself, Admiral, there was no way you could have known that was their plan."

"It was my job to know. I should have seen it coming. They miscalculated one thing though."

Mr. Black asks, "What's that, Admiral?"

"What the magnitude of our response will be."

Ms. Norata asks, "The magnitude of our response?"

Nathan straightens up and looks at her with dread in his eyes and says, "Yes, our response will be absolute. The EDF has protocols in place for situations like this. The president will order me to wipe out the Xandurians, eliminating the threat."

A few minutes later, Admiral Anderson comes back in and says, "Admiral, I have dispatched messages to President Siebert and to the rest of the fleet as you requested."

"Thank you, Admiral."

"I have Lieutenant Green waiting outside to show you all to the guest quarters when you are ready. I've had your quarters prepared and stocked with everything you'll need until we get back to Earth."

"Thank you, Admiral. I guess there's nothing more to do for now. Keep me apprised of any new information."

"Of course, Admiral Stone."

Nathan and his crew exit the holographic battle control center and Lieutenant Green guides them to their quarters on level forty.

As Nathan enters his quarters, he notices that Ms. Norata is once again in the quarters next to his. In light of what happened earlier today, Nathan expects that she will seek him out for comfort and a shoulder to cry on. So, as he is walking by, on his way to the bar, he unlocks the pass-through door that connects his quarters to the quarters next to his.

Nathan finds three bottles of a rather nice twenty-five-year-old single malt scotch sitting on the bar, compliments of Admiral Anderson. He grabs a short tumbler, pours himself a generous amount of scotch and takes a big gulp. Nathan takes the bottle of scotch over to the sitting area, puts it on the coffee table and plunks himself down on the couch. The scotch is delicious and before he knows it, his glass is empty, so he pours himself another.

He leans back into the couch and lets his head fall back so he is looking up at the ceiling. His mind wanders, and that's when the faces of some of the crew of the Invincible enter his thoughts. Some he knew well, others just in passing. Nathan has never lost a command before. He has lost people under his command before, but not an entire crew and ship. Fifteen thousand souls were lost on the Invincible alone.

Before too long, his glass is empty again, so he pours himself another glass, and then another, and another after that. Soon the bottle and his glass are empty, so he opens a second bottle.

The more he drinks, the clearer the faces appear in his mind, the lower he sinks. With the amount of alcohol flowing through his system, it is doubtful that Nathan will remember what triggered the outburst. Was it one face? Was it a few? Was it a memory of something that happened on the Invincible? When it hit, the urge was uncontrollable. Scotch bottles hurled across the room, smash into hundreds of pieces. The glass tumbler following soon after. The coffee tabletop smashed, sending sparks flying from the destroyed holographic display. The coffee table flipped into the air, completing several full revolutions before landing and smashing on the floor.

As he moves around the room, destroying anything he can get his hands on, the sound of a man screaming in the distance suddenly registers in his scotch-soaked consciousness. As he continues, his mind tries to determine where the screaming is coming from. The scream seems to be getting louder. It's not until he turns to throw a decorative crystal orb at a mirror, that he realizes the scream he is hearing is coming from within him. He sees his reflection in the mirror, arm cocked back to throw the orb, mouth wide open, the expression of a man gone mad on his face.

Just as suddenly as it started, his rampage stops. He stands there motionless for a few seconds, panting heavily like he just sprinted a mile. Then he drops to his knees and cries.

That's when he feels a hand touch his shoulder.

He looks to the right to see Ms. Norata moving towards him. She falls to her knees and wraps her arms around him. He falls into her, his head resting on the top of her chest, and begins to sob. She puts the side of her jaw on the top of his head and holds him tight until the alcohol claims him for the night.

CHAPTER 7 – ORDERS

Three days later, the battle group arrives back at Earth. Nathan sees a bright blue flash of light through the windows in his quarters and Earth instantly appears as the Aurora drops out of FTL. He is awake early this morning for a meeting with President Siebert, a meeting that he is not looking forward to.

After showering, Nathan puts on his dress blue uniform with all his medals and ribbons on display and then meets Ms. Norata, Mr. Bell, Mr. Black and Mr. Nagata for breakfast in the officers' mess. They too are wearing their dress blue uniforms for their meeting with the president. It is a quiet breakfast, nobody feels very social this morning.

When they're finished, the five of them head for the elevators and take one down to the internal tram. They then board a tram and are whisked away at high speed to the landing bay. When the tram arrives in the already bustling landing bay, Nathan and his party step off the tram and make their way to the center of the huge bay where a shuttle is standing by to take them down to the planet.

As they approach the shuttle, the pilot salutes Nathan and says, "Good morning, Admiral Stone. I'm Lieutenant Robins, I'll be your pilot this morning. Please, everyone, climb aboard, take your seats and we'll depart as soon as you're ready."

Nathan returns the young lieutenant's salute and says, "Thank you, Lieutenant Robins."

Nathan and his party climb into the shuttle, take their seats and strap in. When everyone is in, Lieutenant Robins climbs aboard and closes the door.

"What is your destination today, Admiral?"

"Earth World Council Tower in London."

"Very good, sir. We'll lift off as soon as I have clearance."

A few minutes later the passengers hear the shuttle's engines throttle up and the shuttle lifts off the deck. It turns ninety degrees to port and moves towards the huge landing bay doors. A few seconds later the shuttle passes through the landing bay's atmospheric force field and out into space.

Lieutenant Robins noses the shuttle over and begins his descent into the atmosphere. Nathan looks out his window to see that big blue marble below, a sight he never tires of seeing. Shortly, the shuttle is descending over the Atlantic Ocean, approaching the west coast of England.

As they approach Earth World Council Tower in London, Lieutenant Robins slows the shuttle down to a crawl and banks to starboard slightly to line it up with the helipad. Soon the shuttle is hovering at two hundred feet directly over the helipad. Lieutenant Robins pulls back on the throttles and the ship descends slowly until it touches down.

Nathan stands up and says, "Nice smooth landing, Lieutenant Robins."

"Thank you, Admiral."

"All right everyone, let's go."

One by one they all exit the shuttle and step out onto the helipad. Just as before, Nathan and his crew can see two British Secret Service agents standing just inside the glass doors, waving them over.

Nathan says, "All right everyone, follow me."

As they enter one agent says, "Admiral Stone, we have been ordered to escort you to President Siebert's office. Would you follow us please?"

"Lead the way, gentlemen."

The other agent walks over to the elevator and places his hand on a biometric hand scanner. The scanner turns green, a bar of white light runs from the tips of his fingers to the heel of his palm, and then displays a message that says, "Access Granted Agent David Hall."

The elevator doors open and everyone steps in. The agent pushes the button for the ninetieth floor, the doors close and the elevator begins its short descent, down two levels. When the doors open, they see four armed soldiers standing guard at the sliding glass doors that lead into the offices of the president and his staff.

The same agent walks over to the glass doors and places his hand on another biometric hand scanner. After scanning his hand, the scanner grants him access. The glass doors slide open and everyone walks into the reception area with the woman sitting behind the large, molded, curved desk.

The woman, dressed in a white business suit, walks out from behind the desk with a tablet in her right hand. Just as before, she is holding the tablet pressed against her chest.

She approaches the group and says, "Admiral Stone, you and your crew can follow me. I will take you in to see the president."

"Very well, lead the way."

The woman takes them down the short hallway to the right of her desk. She knocks on the door, opens it and walks in. Over her shoulder Nathan can see President Siebert sitting behind his desk.

The woman says, "Mr. President, I have Admiral Stone and party to see you, sir."

The president stands up and walks around in front of the desk while saying, "Yes, please come in, Admiral Stone."

Nathan and his crew walk into the president's office and then the woman in the white business suit exits the office, closing the door behind her.

The five officers snap to attention and salute the president.

He returns their salute and says, "At ease everyone."

The president extends his hand to Nathan and says, "Good to see you again, Admiral. Good to see you all."

Nathan shakes the president's hand and says, "Thank you, Mr. President, it's good to see you as well, sir."

"My condolences on the loss of the Invincible, Admiral. She was a fine ship with an outstanding crew. I'm happy that you and your party were not aboard when the Xandurians attacked."

"Thank you, Mr. President."

"Truly shocking that we lost so many lives and four warships, including two of our largest, in the blink of an eye."

"Indeed, sir."

"Now the question is, Admiral, what do we do about it?"

"That's why we're here, Mr. President."

The president gestures with his right hand towards the sitting area in his office and says, "Let's all have a seat, shall we?"

Nathan's four officers have a seat on the couches, Nathan and the president sit down in the two armchairs. The president pulls open a small drawer in the table beside him and pulls out a box of cigars. He offers Nathan and his officers a cigar. They all politely decline. The president takes one and puts the box back in the drawer. He clips the end, lights the cigar and takes a long drag off it. The president pauses for a few seconds and then exhales the smoke.

With smoke tendrils swirling around his face the President says, "They're not going to stop, you know that don't you?"

"Beg your pardon, Mr. President?"

"The Xandurians, they will never stop their quest to be the most powerful race in the galaxy."

"I think we can agree that that will never happen, Mr. President. We've already destroyed ninety percent of their fleet. They are no match for us."

Exhaling another swirling cloud of smoke, “That may be true, but they've proven they can hurt us, and I won't let that happen again. We have to protect our people and our fleet. The only way to do that is to remove the Xandurians from existence.”

“Don't you think that's a bit extreme, Mr. President?”

“Our intelligence services tell me that the Xandurian supreme leader is the driving force behind all the problems we've had lately. He's basically an ego-maniacal dictator with delusions of grandeur, hell bent on conquering the entire galaxy and ruling it with an iron fist. He's got their entire population's support behind him in his fantasy.”

“Mr. President, history has shown that most people who live in a dictatorship go along with what their leader says just to survive. They know they'll be killed if they oppose him. It's possible that if we remove their supreme leader, we can reason with them.”

“I'm not willing to take that chance, Admiral. The only way to guarantee Earth's safety is to wipe them out, every last one of them.”

“With all due respect, Mr. President, genocide is never an option, it's the most heinous of crimes. I agree we need to remove the threat, but we can do that by targeting their government and their military. Killing innocent civilians, women and children is unnecessary, immoral and wrong. We would be no better than them.”

The president takes another drag from his cigar and exhales the smoke quickly. He sits forward in his chair and points the two fingers holding his cigar at Nathan, smoke swirling up from the tip of the cigar, and says with a mixture of anger and ego in his voice, “With all due respect, Admiral Stone, you don't make the decisions around here, I do, and I've made mine. You follow the orders you are given and I'm giving you one. You are to take the bulk of the fleet into Xandurian space where you will destroy all their military installations and wipe out their home world. Now if you won't follow my orders, I can relieve you of your command and get somebody in here that will. It's your choice."

Nathan's officers can't believe what they have just witnessed. They are watching Nathan, eyes wide open, not saying a word, waiting intently for his decision.

Ms. Norata notices that Nathan's face has turned a little red, his hands have tensed to where his fingers are almost tearing through the fabric on the arms of the chair, that the muscle fibers in his jaw and neck have tensed up and are pulsating, he has tilted his head down to the point where he is looking menacingly through his eyebrows at the president. If looks could kill.

Nathan takes a few moments to choose his words carefully, gritting his teeth he says, "You are correct, Mr. President. You give the orders and I follow them."

The president sits back in his chair and says, "I had a feeling you'd see it my way, Admiral."

Still gritting his teeth together, he says, "If there is nothing else, Mr. President?"

"There is one more thing, Admiral Stone. You will need a new flagship. I have already informed Admiral Jameson that you will be taking command of the new battle carrier. I've also taken the liberty of having its registry changed from Vengeance to Invincible. The new Invincible will be ready to leave in a few days. Admiral Jameson was not happy about it, but he saw things my way in the end. In the meantime, I will have all the intelligence our agencies have gathered sent over to you so you can formulate your plan of attack."

Still fighting to control his emotions, Nathan somehow manages to croak out, "Thank you, Mr. President."

"That is all, Admiral Stone."

Nathan and his officers stand, snap to attention and salute. The president stands and returns their salute, after which they turn and follow Nathan out of the president's office.

The British Secret Service agents escort Nathan and his party back to the elevators and up to their shuttle. Nobody says a word. They know Nathan is very angry and that he will want to discuss what just happened out of the ear shot of any junior officers.

When Nathan boards the shuttle he says, "Lieutenant Robins, set your course for my home in Jasper, Alberta, Canada. You'll find the exact coordinates in your navigational computer. Get us there ASAP."

"Very good, sir. We'll lift off as soon as I have clearance."

A few minutes later the passengers hear the shuttle's engines throttle up and the shuttle lifts off the helipad. It turns one hundred and eighty degrees and accelerates rapidly out over the Atlantic Ocean.

After a few minutes Lieutenant Robins says, "Admiral Stone, we've reached thirty thousand feet and our maximum cruising speed. I should have you in Jasper in approximately one hour and twenty minutes, sir."

"Excellent, thank you, Lieutenant Robins."

The flight across the Atlantic is perhaps the quietest flight any of them have ever been on. Nathan sits quietly staring out the window and the others sit in silence not knowing what to make of the meeting they just had with the president.

When they land on Nathan's helipad in Jasper close to an hour and a half later, Nathan and his party exit the shuttle and step out onto the helipad.

Nathan turns back and says, "Lieutenant Robins, you can return to the Aurora. Another shuttle will pick us up here in the morning and take us up to the new Invincible."

Lieutenant Robins gives Nathan a quick salute and says, “Aye sir,” then closes the shuttle door. He lifts off as soon as everyone is clear of the helipad. In a matter of ten seconds the shuttle is out of sight.

Nathan unlocks the door and they all head into the house. They remove their dress uniform jackets, grab beers out of the fridge and head out onto the deck. They all grab a seat around the fire pit and look at Nathan as if to ask what the plan is.

“Okay, now that nobody else is around to hear this, I don’t care what that fucking idiot politician says, I will not be responsible for the mass genocide of the Xandurian people, nor do I want to be labeled as a war criminal. I agree something needs to be done to stop the Xandurians, but I think we can come up with something better than mass murder. In the end I agreed to follow his orders so I can keep control of the situation. If I let him relieve me of duty, he would have put someone in place that would blindly follow his orders, however immoral and illegal they are.”

His four officers all breathe huge sighs of relief and take sips of their beers. They knew that Nathan would never follow such an order but needed to hear he has a different plan.

“Before we go any further, I need to inform you that this is mutiny we are talking about and if we do this our days in the EDF are over for good. We could face incarceration or even the death penalty. Does everybody understand that?”

Ms. Norata says, “Admiral, I think I speak for everyone here when I say that we would rather spend the rest of our days in prison with a clear conscience than to live the rest of our days with the blood of billions of innocents on our hands.”

Mr. Bell stands up, holds up his beer and says, “Here, here.”

The others stand and clink their bottles together, toasting their agreement and then take a drink.

Mr. Black says, “Okay, Boss, what’s the plan?”

"I'm working on it, I'm working on it. Let's head inside and review the intelligence reports that the president sent over."

The five of them head inside to the media room. Nathan opens the encrypted data file that the president sent over. A detailed map of Xandurian space appears on the video screen. The map shows four military bases, on four different planets, each with a shipyard in orbit. It includes a military space station in orbit around a ringed, blue gas giant, their home world, Xandur and the location of the twenty or so remaining Xandurian warships. Ten of those warships are in orbit around Xandur. The other ten are spread thinly between the other military installations.

After a closer examination of the details displayed with each planet, Nathan says pointing to each one, "It appears as if the four planets with the shipyards in orbit are deserted save for the small military bases. There are no civilians present so those are easy targets. We can destroy them from orbit and then take out the shipyards and the sentry ships. Looks as if the space station is also a purely military installation, no civilians present."

Nathan zooms the map in on Xandur and says, "Now Xandur on the other hand, Xandur will be a challenge. There are more than a dozen military bases all over the planet and a mostly civilian population with numbers around the eight billion mark. It will take some careful planning to take out their military bases and very possibly their government buildings, while minimizing civilian casualties."

Nathan zooms the map back out and says, "Each one of you take one of the planets with the military bases and the shipyards and read every bit of intelligence they've provided. I don't want any surprises. I'll take the space station and Xandur. Let's meet back in here in two hours to start formulating our plan of attack."

All four of them stand and say, "Aye sir," in unison and then head to their old bedrooms to go over the intelligence.

Two hours later, the five of them meet back in the media room to go over the details of each military installation and to formulate their plan.

Nathan begins by asking, "Did any of you find anything unexpected or unusual about any of the military bases or shipyards?"

Each of them tells Nathan they found nothing unusual, that it should be no problem at all for a standard size battle group to go in and wipe out the bases and shipyards in under half an hour, and that the shipyards' defenses are no match for the EDF fleet's primary weapons systems.

"Excellent, that's what I like to hear. I found the same thing with the space station, nothing unusual there. Xandur however is going to be a little more challenging. Not at all impossible, just a little more challenging."

After pausing for a minute to think Nathan continues, "So what I propose is we start by deploying a battle group to each of the four planets with a base and a shipyard. We initiate a total communications blackout, jamming both military and civilian communications before we strike. We take out the bases on the surface with orbital nuclear bombardment, then obliterate the shipyards and the sentry ships with our main laser cannon batteries."

"Next, all four battle groups will converge on Xandur. Battle group alpha will stop and take out their space station en route to Xandur. We will approach the planet with our cloaking devices engaged and reveal our presence once all four battle groups have arrived and are in position. As soon as we drop our cloaks, we will take out the ten warships in orbit. Pretty straight forward so far?"

All four of them answer Nathan with, "Yes sir."

"Excellent. Now as far as their government is concerned, I discovered that, well there isn't one. Their supreme leader dissolved their representative form of government a few years ago and made himself a dictator, ruler over all. Coincidentally, shortly after that is when our problems started. From what I can tell, if we take him and his military leadership out, all aggression towards Earth will cease."

Ms. Norata asks, "How are you going to take him out?"

With a little bit of an evil grin Nathan says, "Oh, I've come up with something special for him, don't you worry, Ms. Norata. We shall have vengeance for everyone we have lost."

Mr. Bell asks, "So then last, but not least are the military bases on Xandur. What's your plan for them?"

"Well, I'm still contemplating what to do there. So far all I have come up with is carpet bombing them out of existence, but the civilian casualties would probably be high so I'm still working on that. I still have a few days to think yet."

Mr. Black says, "We know you'll come up with something, sir."

Ms. Norata says, "Now tell us more about what you have planned for their supreme leader."

"Mmmmm sorry, Ms. Norata, you'll just have to wait and see. I can promise you that all of you will have a front row seat. Tomorrow morning we'll head up to the new Invincible to get settled in and to be briefed on her new systems. I can't say I'm looking forward to seeing Admiral Jameson tomorrow, I think he's going to be pretty pissed, but I am looking forward to seeing the new ship."

Mr. Nagata pipes up and says, "I second that, Admiral. I can't wait to check out her engineering section."

"You'll definitely get your chance, Mr. Nagata. I will have a shuttle here tomorrow morning at 09:00 hours to transport us up. For now, let's have a few more beers and then later throw some steaks on the barbecue for dinner."

CHAPTER 8 – THE NEW BATTLE CARRIER

The next morning, Nathan is awakened at 07:00 hours by the gentle sounds of a Zen melody. He opens his eyes, rolls over and touches the glass touch panel top of his nightstand. The touch panel illuminates, a holographic display appears above the nightstand displaying his schedule and his incoming messages. The Zen melody stops playing and the lights in his room power up slowly to a gentle yellowish hue, just enough to see without hurting his eyes.

He gets up and starts his morning routine, after which he heads to the kitchen for coffee and to make breakfast. He is really looking forward to seeing the new battle carrier this morning, but at the same time he is not looking forward to speaking with Admiral Jameson. Even though Nathan had nothing to do with his command being taken away from him, Nathan expects a cold reception from him.

One by one, the other four file into the kitchen looking for coffee to wake them up. When they have finished eating breakfast, they all head back to their rooms to get dressed. The shuttle to take them up to the new Invincible will arrive in less than forty-five minutes.

Before long Nathan hears the shuttle approaching and says, “The shuttle is here, let’s move it people.”

A few minutes later they exit the house, Nathan locks the door and they all head over to the helipad to board the waiting shuttle.

As they board, the pilot salutes and says to Nathan, “Good morning, Admiral Stone, I’m Lieutenant Garcia. I’ll be taking you up to the Vengeance, I mean, the Invincible this morning.”

“Thank you, Lieutenant Garcia. Answer me this Lieutenant, on a scale of one to ten, how pissed is Admiral Jameson?”

“Ummmm, seventy-five, sir.”

"That bad, huh?"

"Yes sir."

"Great."

When everyone has taken their seat and strapped in, Lieutenant Garcia closes the door.

Nathan says, "Okay we're in, Lieutenant, let's get going."

"Aye sir. We'll lift off as soon as I have clearance."

A minute later the passengers hear the shuttle's engines throttle up and the shuttle lifts off the helipad. The pilot pulls the nose up, rams the throttles wide open and heads for space. The G-forces are pushing everyone back in their seats.

Mr. Bell has a big grin on his face and says, "Yeehaw, Lieutenant Garcia. Attaboy, get on it. Wooooh!"

Lieutenant Garcia also has a rather large grin on his face.

The other four look at Mr. Bell, then at each other, smile and shake their heads. This pilot and Mr. Bell are definitely cut from the same cloth.

It only takes a couple of minutes for the shuttle to reach space. After escaping Earth's gravity, Lieutenant Garcia radios the Invincible and requests deactivation of the cloaking device. When the Invincible becomes visible, he turns the shuttle and points it towards the huge battle carrier. Through the front windows Nathan and his crew can see a large flat gray ship off in the distance.

Nathan asks, "Lieutenant Garcia, how far away is the carrier?"

"Roughly, one hundred and twenty-five thousand kilometers, Admiral."

"A hundred and twenty-five thousand kilometers? She looks huge even from this distance."

"Yes sir. She's one and a half times the size of the first-generation battle carrier. Roughly the same length as our new dreadnoughts, just a lot taller and wider. She's a lot sleeker and more modern looking as well, Admiral. She's one hell of a ship, sir."

"I'm sure she is, Lieutenant. I'm sure she is."

As the shuttle approaches, the new battle carrier keeps getting bigger and bigger. Nathan and the others are glued to the windows trying to take the whole thing in and comprehend the size of the ship.

Nathan says, "Lieutenant Garcia, can you fly a slow circle around the carrier so we can get a good look at her?"

"I should be able to sir. Just let me get permission from Invincible's air traffic control."

A minute later the lieutenant says, "Invincible's air traffic control has given me permission for a slow circle around the ship, Admiral. Here we go."

"Excellent, thank you Lieutenant."

The lieutenant spouts off some details about the new carrier, "She is two point three miles long, a mile wide and almost half a mile high. Almost exactly one and a half times bigger than the first-generation battle carrier. Everything else has increased by that same factor. She has one and a half times the laser cannon turrets, rocket launchers, crew, fighters, thrusters and anti-aircraft turrets. She is one formidable ship, Admiral."

"She sure is, Lieutenant Garcia. Look at how sleek and modern she looks too. Amazing."

"Yes sir, it is a totally new and modern design compared to the first generation."

The others sit quietly amazed at the size of the new ship. They're glued to their windows with their mouths hanging open. They can't believe what they are seeing with their own eyes.

After Lieutenant Garcia completes the circle of the carrier, he lines the shuttle up with shuttle bay alpha from the port side.

As the shuttle passes through the atmospheric force field, Nathan and his party notice how unbelievably big the shuttle bay is. It is home to an amazing number of different shuttles and support vehicles housed in, for lack of a better term, shelving units, stacked six units tall all along the shuttle bay's walls. There are literally hundreds of smaller ships neatly stacked everywhere.

Nathan watches as a huge, rail mounted robotic arm rotates around, grabs a shuttle, pulls it out of its cubby hole and sets it gently down on the deck. He also notices that there are several of the robotic arms moving around the bay either pulling ships out of or putting ships into the shelving units.

Nathan thinks to himself, "Very efficient. We can store so many more ships and access them quicker. Brilliant."

With a metallic clang, Lieutenant Garcia sets the shuttle down on the deck and opens the shuttle door.

Nathan and his crew get up to exit the shuttle and, on his way out, Nathan says, "Thank you for the tour, Lieutenant Garcia."

The lieutenant salutes Nathan and says, "My pleasure, Admiral Stone."

Upon exiting the shuttle, Nathan looks across the huge shuttle bay to see Admiral Jameson and a party of five of his officers walking briskly towards them. As expected, Admiral Jameson looks pretty angry.

When Admiral Jameson and his party reach Nathan, they stop, snap to attention and salute him.

Nathan returns their salute.

Admiral Jameson says, "Welcome aboard the Vengeance, I mean, the Invincible, Admiral Stone. If you follow me, I will escort you to the bridge."

"Lead on, Admiral Jameson."

The two parties head across the shuttle bay to the tram station. They board a tram and Admiral Jameson touches the island on the tram's diagram. The doors close, the tram starts to move and whisks them away at high speed towards the center of the huge battle carrier. Before too long, the tram slows down, and it pulls into the stop for the island. When the tram stops, the doors open, everyone gets off and heads over to a group of elevators. They all get in one elevator and Admiral Jameson pushes the button that says bridge on it. The elevator rises at a substantial speed. Before too long, the elevator stops, the doors open, and everyone steps out onto the bridge.

The ship's computer announces in its female voice, "Admiral on the bridge."

Everyone stands and snaps to attention.

Admiral Jameson says, "At ease everyone."

Everyone takes their station again.

As Nathan and his party look around the bridge, they notice that it is very similar to the bridge on the dreadnought Aurora. Almost the entire bridge is finished in the same glossy white polycarbonate. The walls, the support beams, the roof, even the floor is made of the same gloss white material though it is coated with a non-slip material.

All the consoles and chairs are sleek gloss white polycarbonate with molded curves everywhere and all the touch screen displays are finished in gloss black with all the control interfaces displayed in a medium blue that glows just slightly.

All the lighting in the bridge is hidden and recessed, with the majority of the lighting being bright white, there are blue ribbons of light encircling the base of every console and chair on the bridge.

There are several holographic displays active at different stations on the bridge, the largest being at the CAG's station.

His holographic display shows the battle carrier at the center, and the sixty or so F-114 Tomcat fighters currently on patrol, making up the carrier's defensive umbrella.

Nathan walks over to the port side bridge windows and looks out over the massive flight deck, totally blown away by the sheer size of this ship. Looking back, he remembers feeling the same way when he took command of the original Invincible.

He is quickly brought back to reality when Admiral Jameson says, "CAG, bring the fighters home."

"Aye sir."

"Tactical, as soon as the fighters are back aboard re-engage the cloaking device."

"Aye sir."

At this point Nathan decides it's time to deal with the elephant in the room. Not something he is really looking forward to, but knows it is necessary.

He walks over to Admiral Jameson, leans in close and asks in a hushed tone, "Is there somewhere we can go to speak privately?"

The momentary cold stare from Admiral Jameson told Nathan everything. The blatant lack of politeness and respect for his superior in his response confirms Nathan's suspicion.

"Follow me."

Admiral Jameson leads Nathan towards a door just behind and to the right of the commanding officer's station. As they approach, the door slides open. Admiral Jameson skips proper protocol and strides right into the room instead of stepping aside and giving way to his superior.

Nathan is well versed on reading people's body language and from what he is seeing, Admiral Jameson is really pissed. Every muscle in his upper body is tense, his fists are clenched tight and even his gate is angry.

When Nathan enters the room, the door slides shut behind him. There is a large sleek white desk with several chairs sitting in front of it, opposite the door. On the credenza behind the desk, in a glass display case, is a highly detailed, six-foot-long model of the new battle carrier. There are several bookshelves on the back wall of the room and Nathan notices they are loaded with every classic title you can think of. Obviously, this is Admiral Jameson's bridge office.

Admiral Jameson walks over to the front of the desk, turns to face Nathan, crosses his arms and leans back against the edge of the desk, almost to the point of sitting on it straight legged. He doesn't say a word. He just continues to stare at Nathan with a very angry look on his face.

Nathan walks over behind the desk to look at the model of the new battle carrier. He bends at the waist to inspect the model, taking in all the details.

Finally, Nathan breaks the silence, "Quite the ship you have here. Sleek and beautiful, yet powerful and formidable."

In a very disrespectful tone, Admiral Jameson says, "Why don't you just get to the point... SIR."

Nathan walks around back in front of him, crosses his arms, looks him straight in the eyes and in his command voice says, "Very well, I will. I know you're pissed about losing your command. I don't blame you, I would be too. I don't like how the president handled this situation any more than you do, but this is the hand we've been dealt. The fact of the matter is we have a mission to carry out and you have a choice to make. You can stay on board and help complete the mission or you can pack your belongings and take the next shuttle back to Earth. It's your choice. Is that to the point enough for you, mister?"

Admiral Jameson stands up, stares coldly at Nathan for a few moments and then walks around him towards the door. The door slides open as he approaches, but he pauses before walking out of the room.

Without turning back, he says, "I'll be taking a shuttle down to the planet. I will collect my personal effects when you get back from your mission... SIR."

Again, forgoing proper protocol, Admiral Jameson simply walks out, and the door slides closed behind him.

The admiral's reaction doesn't surprise or phase Nathan at all. He didn't expect the admiral to stay on board and help complete the mission. His alpha male ego would not allow him to remain and be seen as a lesser man in the eyes of his crew. It's probably for the best that he made the choice to leave, anyway. The upcoming mission will be difficult enough, conflict with another command level officer on the bridge during battle is a distraction that Nathan doesn't need.

Nathan waits for a few moments before walking out of the office and back out onto the bridge. He has one more unpleasant bit of business before continuing his mission.

Nathan walks to the center of the bridge and says, "Attention everyone. For the duration of this mission the following bridge officers are relieved of duty. The officers that accompanied me aboard will be taking your positions. If you hear your position called out, please stand and leave the bridge immediately. You will remain aboard ship in an off-duty status unless called upon. Is that understood?"

All of the existing bridge crew answer by yelling, "AYE SIR!"

"Very well then, the following officers are hereby relieved. Chief engineer, tactical officer, helmsman and executive officer."

The four officers stand and walk towards the elevators at the back of the bridge. The door opens as they approach, they step on, the doors close and they are gone.

Nathan's officers take the vacated positions. Mr. Nagata takes the chief engineer's station, Ms. Norata takes the tactical station, Mr. Bell takes the helm and Mr. Black, well he stands there looking puzzled.

Nathan looks at him and sees that he doesn't know what to do. Nathan motions for him to come over with his head and eyes.

Mr. Black walks over to Nathan and asks, "Sir?"

"I'm giving you the executive officer position, Mr. Black. I need someone I can trust as my second. This mission is too important. I don't need an XO with misguided loyalties undermining my orders in a critical situation like this."

"But sir, I've never been an XO before."

"Mr. Black, I have all the confidence in the world in you. I know you can do this job. All you have to do is carry out my orders and support my decisions. It's not that difficult."

"Very well, sir, I will do my best."

"I know you will, Mr. Black, I know you will."

Nathan points over his shoulder with his thumb and says, "I'll be in my office, Mr. Black, you have the con."

Nathan goes into his new office and sits down at the large, sleek, white desk. He puts his hand on the black glass top, activating the desk's built in computer system.

The desk scans Nathan's hand and says in the same female voice as the ship's computer, "Access granted, Fleet Admiral Nathan Stone."

Nathan takes his personal tablet out of his pocket and places it on top of the desk. A white rectangle lights up around the tablet to show that the computer is aware of its presence.

"Computer, access my tablet, pull up the file labeled clean sweep and display it using your holographic interface."

"Acknowledged, Admiral."

The holographic interface initializes and displays the different sectors of Xandurian space containing the six targets of this mission. Those being the four planets that have military bases and orbital shipyards, the military space station and last, but not least, the Xandurian home world.

Nathan gives the provided intelligence a final once over before assigning the battle groups a target. Once he is satisfied that he hasn't missed anything, he assigns the targets and begins entering his orders.

Part one of his orders detail the coordination of the communications jam and the simultaneous strikes to take out the shipyards and the bases on the planets they're orbiting.

Part two of his orders detail how all four battle groups will converge on Xandur, with battle group alpha, his battle group, pausing on their way to Xandur, to take out the military space station.

Part three of his orders detail how, once all four battle groups have arrived in orbit around Xandur, they will drop their cloaks and destroy any Xandurian warships in orbit.

Part four of his orders simply state that all commands will hold at that point and no one is to fire on the planet.

After a final read through, he sends a copy of clean sweep to every commanding officer in the fleet and instructs them to form up into their battle groups and get under way immediately.

A few minutes later, Nathan receives confirmation codes from every commanding officer in the fleet acknowledging his orders.

Due to the fact the fleet is cloaked, Nathan can't just go to the bridge windows and watch the fleet jump away.

"Computer, display the fleet's positional data, all ships."

"Acknowledged, Admiral."

The holographic display changes to show Earth and the hundreds of warships in high orbit. Nathan watches as the ships leave orbit and the battle groups begin to form out in open space, with the battle carriers and dreadnoughts in the lead positions.

Soon battle groups beta, charlie and delta jump into FTL and vanish from the display. Only Nathan's battle group, battle group alpha, is left.

Nathan walks back out onto the bridge, sits down in his command chair and says, "Comms, open a channel to the battle group."

"Aye sir, channel open."

"Attention all commands, this is Admiral Nathan Stone on the Invincible. Set your course for our first target and engage your FTL drives. Stone out."

Nathan presses a button on the command console on his chair to close the channel.

"Helm, open the data file I sent you marked clean sweep, set your course and engage the FTL drive, speed 14 TSL."

"Aye sir."

Mr. Bell opens the file, enters the target coordinates into the navigational computer, and initiates the jump into FTL. The huge battle carrier begins to turn.

"Course laid in, coming about to course two-seven-five and engaging the FTL drive."

Once the battle carrier has completed its turn, it accelerates away from Earth rapidly. The bridge crew sees a bright blue flash of light through the bridge windows as the ship accelerates past the speed of light.

A minute later Mr. Bell says, "Admiral, we have reached 14 TSL and are on course for our first target."

"Excellent, thank you, Helm."

"Tactical, verify that all other ships in the battle group have jumped with us."

Ms. Norata does a quick scan and says, “Aye sir, all other ships in the battle group have jumped with us and are on course.”

“Excellent, thank you, Tactical.”

Mr. Black asks, “Helm, what is our time to target?”

“Four days, five hours and forty-six minutes, XO.”

“Thank you, Helm. Admiral, that will give us some time to go through the ships systems and familiarize ourselves with any differences from the first-generation battle carrier.”

Nathan sits back in his chair, looks around the ultra-high-tech bridge and says, “Yes it will, XO. It will indeed.”

CHAPTER 9 – FOUR DAYS TO TARGET

The journey to the Xandurian base seems to be taking forever. To make matters worse, Nathan is hardly sleeping at all. He has orders from the president to eliminate the Xandurian race upon arrival at their home world, orders that don't sit very well with him at all. He knows something has to be done to stop the hostility from the Xandurians, but he does not believe that genocide is the answer.

The Xandurian supreme leader has done away with their representative form of government and set himself up a dictatorship. Previous experience tells him that in most cases, the general population and even the military forces in a dictatorship are forced to do things they don't want to do. They are controlled by threats of violence and fear of retribution if they don't obey the dictator's wishes.

The intelligence the president has provided is not detailed enough to know whether the Xandurian military is being complicit or compliant in the aggression towards Earth. If he were to take out the Xandurian supreme leader, would the Xandurian military leaders have their forces stand down or would they order them to attack? Unfortunately, without more detailed intelligence, Nathan has no way of knowing for sure and he can't take that kind of chance.

He must come up with a plan whereby he can take out the Xandurian supreme leader and the military without harming the civilian population. This is what is keeping Nathan up at night. There are Xandurian military bases in all populated areas of the planet. The military is fully intertwined with the civilian society. So how does he target just the military installations and spare the civilians?

Nathan is also contemplating the consequences for disobeying a direct order from the president. The term "I was just following orders" has been used for centuries by soldiers defending themselves against war crimes charges. Nathan does not intend to put himself in such a position nor does he want the deaths of billions of innocent Xandurian men, women and children on his conscience. He also doesn't relish the thought of being charged with disobeying orders or even mutiny. Either of which would mean the end of his military career, and the penalty could be prison time or even being put to death.

There must be a way to eliminate the threat to Earth that will satisfy the spirit of the president's orders and save the Xandurian race. Nathan is completely preoccupied with finding a solution. It is now day three of the four day journey to the Xandurian base and Nathan has pretty much kept himself in solitude to work on the problem.

He has made several brief appearances on the bridge for status updates, during which, his officers have noticed he is not himself and he does not look well at all.

That night, at about 23:00 hours, Nathan decides he needs to take a break. He needs to go do something else to take his mind off the problem. He changes into a muscle shirt and shorts and heads down to the gym for a workout. When he gets there, he finds the gym is deserted.

After a quick warm up, he decides to work his chest. He walks over to the incline bench, throws two forty-five pound plates on the bar, lies down and does a warmup set. He throws two more plates on the bar and does another set.

He stands up to add yet another two plates to the bar and, out of the corner of his eye, he sees someone else enter the gym. He turns to see Ms. Norata is approaching him with a smile on her face.

As she approaches, she says, "Hey stranger, nice to see you've come out of hiding. Everything okay?"

"Not really. I'm really struggling to come up with a solution for when we reach Xandur. I decided a workout would be a good distraction. Maybe an idea will come to me."

Ms. Norata's eyes gaze up and down Nathan's body, admiring his large, well-defined muscles. She steps a little closer to him and rubs her hand up and down his bare arms and then over his chest.

The look on her face changes to one of pure lust and she says, "I'll bet I could give you a great workout and distract you a hell of a lot more than these weights will."

Nathan's eyes gaze up and down her body admiring her large breasts, that are barely confined by her black sports bra, her thin waist and long legs. He looks up and catches a glimpse of her perfect heart shaped backside in her skintight, tiny, red shorts in one of the mirrors behind her.

He smiles down at her and says, "Oh, I know you could."

She moves closer to him, stands on her tip toes and kisses him aggressively, biting his lip just before breaking the kiss.

Reality hits him for a second, "We can't do this here. We could get caught."

She puts her finger over his lips and says, "SHHHHHH! Don't worry. When I saw you were in here alone, I locked the door. Nobody can come in. Nobody's going to see us."

Nathan smiles and kisses her again. Without breaking the kiss, he picks her up and carries her over to the incline bench he was just using. He lays her down on it and then takes her hands and places them on the weight bar above her head.

"Don't move, I'll be right back."

She smiles up at him and watches him walk over to an equipment rack that's about ten feet away. She sees him grab a skipping rope and then turns around to walk back to her.

When he reaches her, he secures her hands to the weight bar with the skipping rope. He looks down at her and sees a huge smile on her face.

She loves it when he ties her up and uses her body for his own pleasure. She knows this won't be a gentle love making session. She knows what's coming will be rough, hard and fast, exactly how she wants it tonight. Her excitement skyrockets, her heart is racing, her face and chest are flushed, her breathing is shallow and quick, she has broken out in a light sweat and she can feel the wetness between her legs.

When he has finished tying her to the weight bar, he steps around in front of her, so he is standing at her feet. He pulls his muscle shirt off over his head, standing before her in just his shorts.

She looks down and sees the huge bulge in his shorts. She watches intently as he puts his thumbs into the waist band of his shorts, sliding them down his thighs and dropping them to the floor. She sees his large, rock-hard erection spring out and point up towards the ceiling. Her excitement is out of control now, and her mind is screaming for him to hurry up and take her already.

He steps forward, straddling her on the bench, bends down to kiss her, their tongues intertwining, and brings his hands up to her sports bra covered breasts. He squeezes her breasts while continuing to kiss her. Suddenly, without warning, he grabs her sports bra at the middle and with one hard yank, tears it in half, fully exposing her incredible, large breasts. His hands go back to squeezing and massaging her now bare breasts while their mouths continue to make love to each other. After a minute, Nathan breaks the kiss, lowers his head and sucks on her breasts, first one and then the other.

She loves it when he sucks and nibbles on her breasts so as soon as he starts, she lets out a long low moan and pulls at her restraints.

Nathan can't wait anymore. He reaches down, grabs the waist band at the front of her little red nylon shorts and pulls as hard as he can, tearing the flimsy little shorts from her sexy body. He throws the torn shorts to the ground, spreads her legs wide open, positions himself between her legs, places the head of his rock-hard erection at her opening and rams it all the way inside her in one swift, hard thrust.

She screams out in pain from the sudden intrusion, but quickly adjusts to Nathan's size. Not a moment too soon, as Nathan almost immediately begins thrusting in and out of her. He brings his hands up to hold her breasts, lowers his head and sucks one of her nipples into his mouth. He nibbles and sucks on one and then switches to the other. At the same time, he increases the speed and strength of his thrusts until he is ramming into her as hard and fast as he can.

Beneath him, Ms. Norata's senses are on overload. He is taking her like an animal, hard rough and fast, while sucking and biting on her nipples, two of her favorite things. She is moaning loudly and quickly approaching her first orgasm. Nathan bites down on one of her nipples just a little bit harder and that sends her over the edge. She screams at the top of her lungs as she climaxes.

Nathan quickly clamps his right hand over her mouth to muffle her screams. He wouldn't want someone to hear her screaming, they can't afford to get caught. He continues pounding into her as hard and fast as he can.

She is having one orgasm after another as a result of his onslaught. Just as she recovers from one, another one hits. Her eyes have rolled back in her head and she is babbling incoherently through the palm of Nathan's hand.

Nathan is covered in sweat and can feel his orgasm starting to build. Unbelievably, he increases the speed of his thrusts as he approaches orgasm. He moans loudly as the spasms begin and he rams himself deep inside her as he climaxes.

It takes them a few minutes to recover from their intense orgasms and catch their breath. Nathan stands up, walks around the bench, unties Ms. Norata's hands and then hands her a fresh towel.

Nathan realizes they have a small problem. They are in the gym several decks below their staterooms, and Ms. Norata has nothing to wear. He savagely tore off her sports bra and shorts, destroying them, without thinking. The towels in the gym are basically hand towels and are in no way big enough to wrap around her.

"Uh, what are we going to do about clothes to get you back up to your stateroom?

Teasingly, Ms. Norata smiles and says, "Bah, I'm just going to walk naked through the corridors. Nobody will see me."

Nathan is not sure if she's teasing him or not, she can be pretty bold, so he's not sure how to respond.

She can tell by the look on his face that he's not sure if she's teasing him, so she laughs and says, "Relax, I have a white bathrobe in my locker in the change room. I'll go grab it."

Nathan chuckles and breathes a big sigh of relief as she walks off towards the change room. Nathan puts his muscle shirt and shorts back on and then turns around to see Ms. Norata coming back wearing the fluffy, white bathrobe.

She walks over, kisses Nathan and says, "I'll go first, you follow in a few minutes, so we aren't seen leaving together. Thanks for the workout."

Nathan smiles as she turns and walks away. He waits a few minutes before he grabs his things and heads back to his stateroom.

When he steps off the elevator he turns to the right, heading for his stateroom. He has to walk past several others before he gets to his. The door to the stateroom next to his is open, so he glances in when he walks past.

He sees Ms. Norata standing just inside the doorway, still wearing the white bathrobe. He likes the fact that she is right next door, remembering their trip to the Xandurian base on the Aurora. Nathan stands there in the corridor thinking to himself how sexy she is.

She smiles seductively at him before untying and dropping the bath robe to the floor, standing naked before him, but before

Nathan can say or do anything, her stateroom door slides closed.

Nathan proceeds to his stateroom and heads inside. As he passes the door that connects his stateroom to Ms. Norata's he pauses for a second, then smiles and unlocks the door, fairly certain that she will visit him again tonight.

He walks over to the bar and pours himself a generous single malt scotch, aged twenty-five years. The scotch was so delicious that it did not last very long. He makes a mental note that he should have another in a little while. Nathan walks into his bathroom, turns the shower on nice and hot, strips off his clothes and steps in. He relaxes under the stream of hot water for a few minutes before closing his eyes and dropping his head to wash his hair.

As the hot water rains over his head, his mind replays what just happened in the gym. As he relives it, his erection returns, and he is soon hard as a rock. He wishes she was in the shower with him right now so he could take her again. He loved tying her up, tearing her clothes off and ravaging her like a wild animal.

He thinks to himself, "She was the perfect distraction, exactly what I needed to take my mind off this problem. She is the key to my problem. Wait, Ms. Norata is the key to my problem? God damn, Ms. Norata is the key to my problem!"

He just begins to say it out loud, "Fuck me, of course, Ms. Norata is...," but stops when he feels someone press up against him from behind. He feels an arm wrap around his mid-section and a hand wrap around his erection.

With his head still under the streaming water, he smiles and thinks to himself, "Wish granted, round two coming up."

CHAPTER 10 – THE XANDURIAN SHIPYARDS

The next day, Nathan's battle group is closing in on their first target, their assigned Xandurian military base and shipyard.

The other three battle groups have already reached their targets, have dropped out of FTL and are awaiting Nathan's signal to jam their communications and attack.

Nathan planned this to be a swift, coordinated, surprise attack, wiping out the four bases, shipyards and any war ships, simultaneously to ensure one base can't warn the others, ruining the element of surprise.

When they are two minutes out Nathan says, "Comms, signal the battle group to go to battle stations and drop out of FTL in sixty seconds."

"Aye sir."

"Mr. Bell, drop us out of FTL in sixty seconds."

"Aye sir."

"XO, sound battle stations."

Mr. Black answers, "Aye sir," and announces over the ship's address system, "Battle stations, battle stations, all hands man your battle stations, this is not a drill."

An alarm sounds after his address and the lights on the bridge change from white to red.

Almost a minute later Mr. Bell says, "Dropping us out of FTL in 5... 4... 3... 2... 1... now."

The massive battle carrier decelerates, and the bridge crew sees a bright blue flash of light through the bridge windows as the ship drops below the speed of light.

Since the battle group dropped out of FTL while cloaked, the Xandurians are not alerted to their presence. It also prevents

Nathan from knowing if the rest of his battle group has dropped out of FTL just by looking out the bridge windows.

“Tactical, has the rest of the fleet dropped out of FTL?”

“Aye sir, all ships have arrived.”

“Excellent, thank you, Tactical.”

Through the front bridge windows, the bridge crew can see the planet, the shipyards with twenty or so ships in different phases of construction, and two sentry warships patrolling close to the shipyards.

“Comms, signal the other battle groups to begin jamming the Xandurian’s communication and then start your communications jam. After that, signal the battle group to move into attack position.”

“Aye sir.”

“Helm, move us into attack position and come to a full stop.”

“Aye sir.”

Nathan has laid out a very detailed plan of attack. The commanding officer of each ship in the four battle groups knows what their target is and what weapons they are to use to destroy it.

The battle carriers will launch a series of nuclear-tipped, tactical missiles to take out the bases on the planets. The entire battle group will then decimate the shipyards, any ships being built, and any patrolling warships, using their laser cannons.

A few minutes later, Mr. Bell brings the huge battle carrier to a full stop and says, “Admiral, we have reached our attack position and have come to a full stop.”

“Thank you, Helm.”

“Tactical, arm six of the nuclear-tipped, tactical missiles, target the base on the surface of the planet and open the launch bay doors.”

"Aye sir, arming the missiles, target locked, and launch bay doors are open. If you would enter your launch codes, Admiral, I can fire the missiles."

"Very well, Tactical," Nathan types his launch codes into his command console, "My launch codes are entered and verified."

"Comms, open a channel to the entire fleet."

"Aye sir, channel open."

Nathan stands and walks a little closer to the main view screen at the front of the bridge, "Attention all commands, this is Admiral Stone on the Invincible, we will begin the attack on my mark. Battle carriers, launch your nukes in 3... 2... 1... mark."

Simultaneously, Nathan turns and points at Ms. Norata to fire the missiles.

She presses the launch buttons for the six missiles. The rocket engines ignite, sending the missiles streaking towards the planet.

Not giving the Xandurians any time to react, Nathan says, "Attention all commands, open fire. Take out the shipyards and the sentry ships."

Immediately, thousands of bright, red laser blasts are streaking through space towards the shipyards and the patrolling sentry ships.

The first few laser blasts aimed at the shipyards obliterate the control tower before they can raise their shields.

The first few laser blasts aimed at the sentry ships impact directly on the hulls before the Xandurians manage to raise their shields. With their shields now up, the Xandurian ships turn towards the cloaked EDF battle group and return fire.

A few minutes after launching the missiles, Ms. Norata says, "Admiral, the nukes have reached their target. Detonation in 3... 2... 1... now."

The bridge crew sees several bright white flashes of light, followed by massive explosions on the planet's surface.

Thirty seconds after the nukes detonate, the shipyard is obliterated by a series of large explosions, leaving nothing but a massive debris field in orbit around the planet. Many of the larger pieces feel the effect of the planet's gravity and begin entering the atmosphere, burning up as they fall.

Ten seconds after the shipyards explode, the shields on the two sentry ships fail. A few seconds after that, both ships disappear in two large explosions.

Nathan looks around the bridge of the Invincible as the crew cheers and celebrates their victory.

When the noise dies down Nathan asks, "Tactical, any other ships in the area or approaching in FTL?"

"Negative, sir, no ships in the area or approaching in FTL."

"Excellent, thank you, Tactical."

With the fleet wide channel still open, Nathan says, "Attention all commands, this is Admiral Stone on the Invincible. We have destroyed our initial targets and are moving on to our secondary target. Battle groups bravo, charlie and delta, report when your initial targets are destroyed. Stone out."

Nathan walks back to his chair and presses a button on the command console on his chair to close the channel.

Next, Nathan says, "Comms, open a channel to the battle group."

"Aye sir, channel open."

"Attention all commands, this Admiral Stone, stand down from battle stations, set course for the Xandurian space station and engage your FTL drives, maximum speed. Stone out."

Nathan presses a button on the command console on his chair to close the channel.

"XO, signal the crew to stand down from battle stations."

"Aye sir."

He grabs the microphone and announces over the ship's address system, "All hands, stand down from battle stations, repeat, all hands stand down from battle stations."

A chime sounds after his address and the lights on the bridge change from red to white.

"Helm, set course for the Xandurian space station and engage the FTL drive, 14 TSL."

"Aye sir, course laid in, engaging the FTL drive, speed 14 TSL."

The huge battle carrier accelerates rapidly away from the planet, and the bridge crew sees a bright blue flash of light through the bridge windows as the ship passes the speed of light.

A minute later Mr. Bell says, "Admiral, we are on course for the Xandurian space station and are traveling at 14 TSL. Estimated time of arrival two hours and forty-two minutes."

"Thank you, Helm, steady as she goes."

"Aye sir."

"Tactical, verify that all other ships in the battle group have jumped with us."

Ms. Norata does a quick scan and says, "Aye sir, all other ships have jumped with us and are on course."

"Excellent, thank you, Tactical."

A minute later the communications officer says, "Admiral, battle groups bravo, charlie and delta, report their initial targets have been destroyed and they are on course for Xandur."

"Excellent, thank you, Comms."

CHAPTER 11 – THE XANDURIAN SPACE STATION

Nathan has been sitting in his command chair quietly for a little over two and a half hours finalizing his plan for when the fleet arrives at Xandur. He is ninety-five percent certain that he can successfully remove the Xandurian supreme leader from power and remove their military capabilities without killing any civilians. The only thing he is worried about is how the president will react to his fleet admiral disobeying a direct order, even though he completed the mission successfully.

Mr. Bell turns and says, “Admiral, five minutes until we arrive at the Xandurian space station.”

“Thank you, Helm.”

“Tactical, how many Xandurian warships are guarding the space station?”

Ms. Norata checks the long-range scanners and says, “There are two sentry ships, sir.”

“Excellent, thank you, Tactical.”

“Comms, open a channel to the battle group.”

“Aye sir, channel open.”

“Attention all commands, this is Admiral Stone. Go to battle stations. We will arrive at the Xandurian space station in three minutes. As soon as we drop out of FTL, target the station, and the two sentry ships and open fire. If everything goes according to plan, we will catch them off guard with their shields down. They won’t last very long after we begin our assault. Stone out.”

Nathan presses a button on the command console on his chair to close the channel.

“XO, sound battle stations.”

Mr. Black answers, "Aye sir," and announces over the ship's address system, "Battle stations, battle stations, all hands man your battle stations, this is not a drill."

An alarm sounds after his address and the lights on the bridge change from white to red.

Once again Nathan sits quietly staring at the main view screen watching the stars streak by.

Two minutes later Mr. Bell says, "Admiral, we are approaching the Xandurian space station. Dropping out of FTL in 5... 4... 3... 2... 1... now."

The battle carrier decelerates, and the bridge crew sees a bright blue flash of light through the bridge windows as the ship drops below the speed of light.

Directly in front of them appears the huge, ringed, blue, gas giant with the space station in orbit. The two sentry ships are silently gliding past, heading in opposite directions just one kilometer off the station.

"Tactical, target the space station and open fire. Fire at will."

"Aye sir, target locked. Firing."

A few seconds later there are thousands of red laser blasts streaking towards the station and the two sentry ships. The first laser blasts hit the ships and the station, impacting directly on the hulls. They don't have their shields up, proving that they have indeed caught the Xandurians completely off guard.

None of the bridge officers on the Invincible, including Nathan, had any idea of how short this battle would actually be. The initial laser blasts that hit the sentry ship closest to the space station, impact directly on the bridge of the ship. With their shields down there was nothing to protect them. The bridge of the ship is gone. Nothing remains except a gaping hull breach.

The subsequent laser blasts push the sentry ship to port, setting it on a collision course with the center of the space station. The section of the space station that houses the reactor.

A split second after the ship crashes into the hull of the space station, the reactor breaches, setting off a massive explosion that instantly vaporizes the sentry ship.

The explosion quickly engulfs the entire station as well, sending out a large shock wave. The shock wave reaches the second sentry ship, which was unable to raise its shields, blowing it into millions of small pieces that are sent spinning outwards in all directions.

Nathan and the other officers on the Invincible's bridge can't believe their eyes. Nobody says a word. The bridge is silent other than the normal electronic noises and some background chatter on the comm system. Nobody expected that the battle would be over in twenty seconds.

Nathan finally blinks and breaks the silence, "Wow!"

He turns to look at Ms. Norata and says, "Nice shooting, Ms. Norata."

Still dealing with disbelief she says, "Thank you, sir."

Nathan turns back to looking at the main view screen and says, "Comms, open a channel to the battle group."

"Aye sir, channel open."

"Attention all commands, this is Admiral Stone. Stand down from battle stations, set course for Xandur and engage your FTL drives, maximum speed."

Nathan presses a button on the command console on his chair to close the channel.

"XO, signal the crew to stand down from battle stations."

Mr. Black answers, "Aye sir," and announces over the ship's address system, "All hands, stand down from battle stations, repeat, all hands stand down from battle stations."

A chime sounds after his address and the lights on the bridge change from red to white.

"Helm, set course for Xandur and engage the FTL drive, 14 TSL."

"Aye sir, course laid in, engaging the FTL drive, speed 14 TSL."

The huge battle carrier turns and accelerates rapidly away from the ringed, blue, gas giant and the bridge crew sees a bright blue flash of light through the bridge windows as the ship passes the speed of light.

A minute later Mr. Bell says, "Admiral, we are on course for Xandur and are traveling at 14 TSL. Estimated time of arrival is two days, four hours and thirty-five minutes."

"Thank you, Helm, steady as she goes."

"Aye sir."

"Tactical, verify that all other ships in the battle group have jumped with us."

Ms. Norata does a quick scan and says, "Aye sir, all other ships have jumped with us and are on course."

"Excellent, thank you, Tactical."

CHAPTER 12 – XANDUR

Forty-eight hours later, Nathan is in Admiral Jameson's office, behind the bridge, working on the final details of his plan.

Over the comm system comes the communication officer's voice, "Admiral, sorry to disturb you. I wanted to let you know that I have just received word from the commanding officers of the other three battle groups. They say they have arrived at Xandur and have settled into a high orbit. Just as reported, there are ten Xandurian warships in orbit around the planet."

"Thank you, Comms, stand by to send my reply."

"Aye sir, standing by."

Nathan switches channels to speak to Mr. Bell.

"Helm, time until we arrive at Xandur?"

"Four hours and thirty minutes, sir."

"Thank you, Helm."

Nathan switches back to speak to the communications officer.

"Comms, send this to the commanding officers of the three battle groups. Destroy the ten warships in orbit and then blockade the planet. Update me at that point. Hold until my arrival. We are four and a half hours out."

"Aye sir, sending your response now."

"Thank you, Comms."

An hour goes by before the communications officer interrupts him again, "Admiral, I have just received a status update from the other battle groups. They said the ten warships have been destroyed, and the fleet has set up a blockade around the planet. Nothing is getting in or out."

"Thank you, Comms. Please send them a standard acknowledgement and let them know we are three and a half hours out."

"Aye sir, sending your response now."

A little over three hours later, Nathan walks back out onto the bridge, sits down in his chair and says, "XO, status report."

Mr. Black answers, "We are on course for Xandur, traveling at 14 TSL. ETA approximately ten minutes. The battle group is still cloaked, sir."

"Thank you, XO."

"Comms, send to all commands in the battle group, disengage your cloaking devices."

"Aye sir."

"Tactical, disengage the cloaking device."

"Aye sir, disengaging cloaking device now."

Several minutes later Mr. Bell says, "Admiral, we are approaching the planet Xandur. Dropping out of FTL in 5... 4... 3... 2... 1... now."

The battle carrier decelerates, and the bridge crew sees a bright blue flash of light through the bridge windows as the ship drops below the speed of light.

The planet Xandur instantly appears through the front bridge windows. The planet appears mostly blue as water covers ninety percent of its surface. There are dozens of small land masses spread out across the surface, and just like Earth the north and south poles are frozen. There are also a lot of clouds floating around in the atmosphere.

Surrounding the planet are the roughly two hundred and forty EDF war ships that make up the blockade, and that number is about to go up.

"Comms, open a channel to the battle group."

"Aye sir, channel open."

"Attention all commands, this is Admiral Stone speaking. I want you to join the rest of the fleet. Take up a position in high orbit around the planet and then hold. Stone out."

Nathan presses a button on the command console on his chair to close the channel.

"Comms, get me Admiral Anderson on the Aurora."

"Aye sir, one moment."

A few moments later the communications officer says, "Sir, I have Admiral Anderson for you."

"Very well, Comms, on screen."

Admiral Anderson appears on the main view screen, standing in the middle of the Aurora's bridge.

"Admiral Stone, what can I do for you, sir?"

"Well, Admiral Anderson, I need an escort."

"An escort, sir?"

With a little smile on his face Nathan says, "Yes. You and I are going to pay the Xandurian supreme leader a little visit. Go to battle stations, engage your cloaking device, fire up your anti-gravity generators and prepare for atmospheric entry. We'll start our descent in one hour."

"Sir, we've never taken the Aurora down into a planet's atmosphere before."

"And I've never taken this generation of battle carrier into a planet's atmosphere either, but there is a first time for everything, wouldn't you agree, Admiral Anderson?"

"We're in a combat situation though, Admiral Stone. Are you sure this is wise?"

The smile is now gone from Nathan's face, "You have your orders, Admiral. I'll send you our destination coordinates shortly."

"Yes sir."

"Stone out."

Nathan presses a button on the command console on his chair to close the channel and shut down the view screen. He opens the file containing the destination coordinates and some simple directions and sends it over to Admiral Anderson.

"XO, sound battle stations."

Mr. Black answers, "Aye sir," and announces over the ship's address system, "Battle stations, battle stations, all hands man your battle stations, this is not a drill."

An alarm sounds after his address and the lights on the bridge change from white to red.

"Helm, fire up the anti-gravity generators."

"Aye sir, bringing the anti-grav generators online now."

"Tactical, engage the cloaking device."

"Aye sir, engaging the cloaking device now."

"CAG, light up the flight deck."

The CAG pauses for a second, wondering what Nathan has planned and then says, "Aye sir, lighting up the flight deck. Engaging the atmospheric force field. Powering up the flight deck lighting, the atmosphere generators, the heaters and the gravity plating. Ten minutes until we have a workable atmosphere, Admiral."

"Very well CAG. As soon as you have a workable atmosphere, I want six full squadrons of Tomcats armed and ready for takeoff on the flight deck. I also want two Tomcats parked right on the bow facing forward. You have fifty-five minutes."

Puzzled regarding the two Tomcats the CAG asks, "Sir?"

"You heard me, mister."

"Aye sir."

"I've cooked up a little surprise for the Xandurian supreme leader."

Nathan starts to walk back towards Admiral Jameson's office behind the bridge, when he pauses, turns and says, "Commander Norata, would you please join me in Admiral Jameson's office? We have something to discuss."

Ms. Norata responds, "Aye sir," then walks towards Nathan.

Nathan holds the door open for her, then follows her in, the door sliding shut behind them.

"What can I do for you, Admiral?"

"Commander Norata, how many nano-missiles do we have at our disposal?"

A little puzzled, she asks, "Throughout the fleet, sir?"

"Yes, how many nano-missiles do we have here at Xandur right now?"

"Well, sir, I don't have an exact number, but if I had to guess I would say roughly two hundred and fifty missiles per ship, three hundred and twenty ships," she pauses to quickly do the math in her head, "I would say right around eighty thousand nano-missiles, Admiral."

"Eighty thousand missiles?"

"Roughly, yes, sir."

"And how many nanites are there in each missile?"

"Standard load is right around ten billion nanites per missile, sir."

"Wow, that's a lot of nanites isn't it?"

"Yes sir."

"And correct me if I'm wrong, but the nanites are quite sophisticated and can be programmed to attack certain systems and leave others alone?"

"That is correct, sir."

"Excellent. In your estimation, do we have enough nanites to flood the atmosphere of the planet below us?"

"Yes sir, that shouldn't be a problem."

"Wonderful."

"Sir, may I ask what you are planning to do?"

"Yes, of course, Commander. As you well know, the president ordered me to wipe out the Xandurians. I don't agree with his order. I will not be responsible for the genocide of an entire race. There are billions of innocent men, women and children down on that planet and I refuse to murder them because of what their leader and their military is foolishly attempting to do."

"I have been wracking my brain to come up with a solution to eliminate the Xandurians that are causing the problem and remove the threat to Earth without wiping out the entire population of the planet."

"I have you to thank, in part, for helping me come up with the solution. The other night, when you, shall we say, took my mind off things for a while..."

Ms. Norata looks down at the floor, smiles and blushes just a little.

"Was the distraction I needed to reset my brain. Taking a break from trying to figure out how to solve the problem worked beautifully. The solution hit me like a ton of bricks in the shower just before you came in and joined me."

Remembering the shower and what happened after that brings a lustful smile to Ms. Norata's face.

"We take out the supreme leader and his military commanders, and then we use our nanites to attack and destroy their military technology, thus eliminating the threat to Earth and keeping the casualties to a minimum."

Ms. Norata smiles and aggressively hugs Nathan, "That's brilliant, Nathan, truly brilliant."

"Thank you, Aleena."

"But, will the president be satisfied with your solution, or will he see it as you disobeyed his orders?"

"I'm not sure how the president will react."

"If he reacts badly, your career in the EDF will be finished. You may even face charges and jail time."

"That's better than living with the blood of billions of innocents on my conscience."

She hugs him again, holds him tight and says, "You're doing the right thing and whatever the outcome, I will be there to love and support you."

He hugs her tighter and says, "Thank you, Aleena."

She smiles, turns and walks towards the door.

"Oh, and Aleena..."

She stops and turns back to look at Nathan.

"I love you too."

She smiles, turns, walks towards the door once again and says over her shoulder, "You better."

The door slides open as she reaches it, she walks out onto the bridge and the door slides closed behind her.

Nathan sits down in the chair behind Admiral Jameson's desk and smiles. That was the first time that either of them said they loved the other.

Nathan stays in the office until his one hour deadline is up. He walks back out onto the bridge and heads over to the port side windows to look down on the flight deck. He sees that the CAG has the six squadrons of Tomcats ready for takeoff and the two additional Tomcats sitting at the bow of the ship. He then walks back over to his chair and sits down.

"Comms, get me Admiral Anderson on the Aurora."

"Aye sir, one moment."

A few moments later the communications officer says, "Sir, I have Admiral Anderson for you."

"Very well, Comms, on screen."

Admiral Anderson appears on the main view screen, standing in the middle of the Aurora's bridge.

"Admiral Anderson, are you ready to descend?"

"Yes sir, we're as ready as we ever will be."

"Relax Admiral, this will be a walk in the park."

"Yes sir, if you say so, sir."

"We're about to start our descent. Follow us down to the coordinates I sent you, take up an over watch position two hundred meters behind and above the Invincible. You are to provide anti-aircraft cover fire should any Xandurian fighters take a run at us after we drop our cloak."

"Understood, sir."

"Excellent. Stone out."

Nathan presses a button on his command console to close the channel and shut down the view screen.

"Helm, take us down into the atmosphere, nice and slow. I don't want anything to alert the Xandurians that we are dropping in on them. I want to see the look of surprise on the supreme leader's face."

"Aye sir, beginning our descent, nice and slow."

Nathan enters the destination coordinates into the computer and sends them over to Mr. Bell.

"Helm, when we are two kilometers from the surface of the planet, I want you to head for the coordinates I just sent you."

"Aye sir."

Nathan activates the main view screen and puts a picture up of a city scape, just off an ocean bay with a bunch of tall, sleek looking skyscrapers.

"At those coordinates you will find this two hundred story, curved, glass covered, skyscraper that is situated right off the ocean in a large bay area."

Nathan zooms the view screen in on the skyscraper in question.

"I want you to approach the building from the west, drop the ship down until the flight deck is level with the top floor and park the bow of the ship twenty feet away from the curved windows."

Mr. Bell lifts his head, looking straight forward with a look of disbelief on his face, then slowly turns and looks at Nathan.

"I beg your pardon, Admiral?"

"I want you to park the bow of the ship twenty feet from the curved windows on the top floor of that building."

"Are you serious, sir?"

"Very serious."

"Just to be clear, you want me to park a spaceship that is two point three miles long, a mile wide, half a mile high, weighing in at oh about two million tons, twenty feet away from the top floor of a skyscraper?"

"That's right."

Mr. Bell turns back around to his control console and says, "Okay then."

Nathan leans forward in his chair, "Are you saying you can't do it, Mr. Bell?"

"Oh, no sir, I can do it. I could do that in my sleep. I can fly anything, anywhere and stop it on a dime. I'm the best pilot there ever was. I just can't believe you're asking me to do it."

Nathan sits back in his chair, smiles and chuckles to himself. He looks over at Mr. Black who is also chuckling. When the two officers' eyes meet, they laugh even harder, fighting to keep quiet. Nathan puts his hand over his mouth and Mr. Black drops his head down, attempting to hide their laughter.

Nathan composes himself and then says, "I'm glad to see that you've been working on your modesty, Mr. Bell."

Not realizing that Nathan is teasing him he says, "Thank you sir, it hasn't been easy."

Nathan says, "I'm sure it hasn't been," then looks at Mr. Black again. Immediately, both men start laughing again.

Roughly twenty minutes after entering the atmosphere, Mr. Bell says, "Admiral, we have reached an altitude of two kilometers and I am heading for the coordinates you provided."

"Thank you, Helm."

Mr. Bell turns the massive battle carrier gently to port, beginning a long, slow, sweeping turn. As the ship turns, it banks about fifteen degrees. Normally the crew wouldn't think about it or even notice, but because they can see a horizon and they are only two kilometers up from the surface of the ocean, it is a little unnerving to most of the bridge crew.

When Mr. Bell completes the turn, the bridge crew can see a large island on the horizon. Nathan switches the main view screen to display the view from the bow of the ship and zooms in on the island. The island is half covered with skyscrapers that are tightly packed together.

The Xandurians have a real flare for interesting architecture. Most of the skyscrapers are beautifully designed with sleek flowing lines and interesting shapes. Front and center is the building Nathan is interested in.

Mr. Bell is approaching the island very slowly. A ship this big can't stop on a dime and the last thing he wants to do is overshoot the building because he underestimated the distance he needs to come to a full stop. After all, his reputation as being the best pilot ever, is on the line.

It takes a little while for the carrier to travel the sixty or so kilometers to the island. Mr. Bell brings the carrier to a full stop about a kilometer away from the building.

"Admiral, we are one kilometer out at an altitude of two kilometers. I'll ease us in the rest of the way using short, controlled thruster bursts. When I get the bow of the ship within twenty feet of the building, I will drop us down so the flight deck is level with the top floor of the building."

"Excellent, thank you, Helm. Proceed."

"Aye sir, here we go."

Mr. Bell nudges the carrier forward using the RCS thrusters. It takes a little while, but eventually he gets the bow of the ship right where it is supposed to be.

"Admiral, the bow of the ship is twenty feet away from the building, however we need to retract the long-range communications antennas on the bow and adjust the forward shield harmonics before I can drop us down into position."

"Comms, retract the bow antennas."

"Aye sir, antennas retracted."

"Thank you, Comms."

"Tactical, pull the forward shields in close to the bow."

"Aye sir, shields pulled in to fifteen feet."

"Thank you, Tactical."

Nathan zooms the bow view on the main view screen out and back to zero magnification. Mr. Bell nudges the carrier straight down using the RCS thrusters. Soon the top of the building appears just over the bow of the ship. A few more nudges with the thrusters and the windows for the top floor come into view.

"Admiral, we are in position, sir."

"Thank you, Helm, well done."

"Thank you, sir. I may need a drink when I'm off duty."

Nathan gets up and walks over to the helm station. He slaps Mr. Bell on the shoulder and says, "Absolutely, I'll buy."

He walks over to the communications station and asks, "Comms, can you hack into their communications network and tie in the translator?"

"Yes sir, absolutely. It'll just take me a few minutes."

Nathan grabs a headset off her console, "When you're done can you patch it through to this headset?"

"Yes sir."

"Excellent, get to it."

"Aye sir."

Nathan walks over to the CAG's station and says, "Get your pilots in their planes. When I order Ms. Norata to drop the cloak, I want them in the air flying a defensive perimeter of ten miles. Nothing gets near the carrier or the dreadnought."

"Aye sir."

Finally, Nathan walks over to the tactical station, "Keep the view screen zoomed in on me. When I turn and point at you, I want you to drop the cloak."

"Aye sir."

"I can't wait to see the look on their leader's face when he sees the largest warship in the galaxy hovering just outside his window."

Ms. Norata smiles and shakes her head a little.

With a slight grin on his face Nathan says, "I'm going for a little stroll, I'll be back in a little while."

"Enjoy your… stroll, sir."

"Thank you, Ms. Norata, I'm sure I will."

Nathan walks to the rear of the bridge, gets in an elevator and takes it down to the flight deck. When he walks out onto the flight deck, he gets in a small electric utility car and drives down the flight deck to the bow of the ship. He parks the car and walks up to the edge of the flight deck, standing between the two Tomcats.

Through the windows in front of him, he can see about a dozen Xandurians sitting at a large, round table. One of them is dressed in civilian looking clothes, so Nathan assumes he is the supreme leader. The others are all dressed in a type of white military uniform, all with what appears to be rank insignia and commendations on their shoulders and chest. Very similar in style to what the EDF does on Earth. Nathan assumes these are the military leaders, the Xandurian generals.

Nathan then turns around and walks over to the two Tomcat pilots that are standing beside their planes waiting for orders. He motions for them to join him for a quick conversation.

"Gentlemen, I want each of you to climb into your cockpits and arm a couple of your missiles. At any point if you see me raise my right hand and snap my fingers, you will immediately fire those missiles into the office behind me. Understood?"

Both pilots answer, "Understood, Admiral."

"Excellent, hop to it."

Again, both pilots answer, "Aye sir," and then run to their planes and climb up into their cockpits.

Nathan turns and walks back up to the edge of the flight deck, puts the headset on and asks, "Are you ready, Comms?"

"Yes sir, patching you through now."

Immediately Nathan can hear the conversation going on in the office in front of him. The generals are informing the supreme leader how they are experiencing interference with their communications and have lost contact with their bases, shipyards, space station and the sentry warships in orbit.

The supreme leader asks, "Are you sure it's just a communications issue, gentlemen?"

One general says, "Yes, Supreme Leader."

"How can you be sure?"

Another of the generals says, "What else could it be? No one would dare to attack us, and we would certainly know if they did."

Nathan's eyes have been opened. The Xandurians' arrogance is unbelievable. It has obviously blinded them and made them think they're invincible. It's time to open their eyes.

Nathan taps a button on the side of his headset to activate the microphone and says, "Forgive the interruption, Supreme Leader, but your generals are wrong. Your bases, your shipyards, your space station and what was left of your fleet have all been destroyed. They are nothing more than dust and debris now."

The supreme leader and the generals look around the room with looks of confusion plastered all over their faces.

The supreme leader asks, "Who is this? Who is speaking? Where are you? How are you listening to our conversation?"

Nathan smiles, he's been anticipating this moment for days.

"My apologies, Supreme Leader, allow me to introduce myself."

Nathan turns momentarily and points at the bridge.

On the bridge, Ms. Norata disengages the cloaking device.

Following suit, Admiral Anderson disengages his cloaking device revealing the Aurora on over watch just above and behind the Invincible.

Nathan relishes in the moment, watching looks of fear, panic and disbelief overtake the twelve incredibly arrogant aliens in front of him as the cloak disengages and the two massive warships appear just outside their office windows.

The Xandurian supreme leader immediately jumps to his feet, sending his chair flying backwards, causing it crash into the wall behind him.

Nathan says, “First off, I don’t want any of you to move. You see, the two fighter jets behind me? I’ve ordered the pilots to launch their missiles if I snap my fingers. Do you understand?”

The supreme leader looks around at his generals and says, “We understand.”

“Excellent,” Nathan holds up his index finger and says, “One moment gentlemen, it’s about to get very noisy.”

Behind Nathan, way down the flight deck, the six squadrons of F-114 Tomcats fire up their engines and lift off the deck. After taking off, they vector off in all directions to set up the ten-mile defensive perimeter that Nathan ordered.

“Sorry about that, that was the carrier’s defensive umbrella taking off and getting into position. I’m sure by now someone in this city has spotted the two huge alien warships hovering in the sky above them and alerted your military. I can’t have your fighters shooting at us now, can I?”

“Can we get to the point please, Admiral Stone?”

“Oh, you know who I am do you, Supreme Leader?”

“Yes, you are Admiral Nathan Stone of the Earth Defense Force and you have been a particular pain in my side for a couple of years now.”

“I’m pleased to meet you too, Supreme Leader. Do you know why I’m here?”

“Yes, you want to kill me.”

"No, if I wanted to kill you, we wouldn't be having this conversation. You, your generals and your office would be one big charred pile of rubble by now."

"Then why are you here?"

"Don't get me wrong, Supreme Leader, the president of Earth sent me here to kill you. Unlike you, I don't enjoy killing, I am giving you a chance to live. I hope to reason with you, to see if I can convince you to give up your hopeless quest to be the most powerful species in the galaxy."

"You're wasting your time, Admiral Stone. I will not stop until we ARE the most powerful species in the galaxy and then I will rule the galaxy with an iron fist."

"You, sir, are delusional if you think you can actually pull that off. You don't have the technology, the resources or, quite frankly, the intelligence to defeat every other military in the galaxy. Even if you managed to, maintaining control over the whole galaxy would be impossible."

"We are destined to rule over all, and we will not stop until we do."

"We? Do all your people believe this craziness?"

"It does not matter what my people believe. I am their supreme leader and they will follow me and do whatever I say."

"Ah yes, a dictator with delusions of grandeur, how original. What about your generals here, what do they believe?"

"It does not matter what they believe, I am the supreme leader and they follow my orders."

"You know, I'm beginning to see the problem here."

"Problem? What Problem?"

"You. You are the problem. I can see there is no reasoning with you. You are a cancer that needs to be cut out if the

Xandurian people are to survive. Goodbye, Supreme Leader. Generals."

Nathan raises his right hand all the way above his head and snaps his fingers.

The twelve Xandurians run for the door, but there is no escape for them now.

The pilots sitting behind Nathan in the two F-114 Tomcats pull the triggers on their flight sticks. Two missiles from each fighter ignite and launch from underneath their wings. It takes less than a second for the missiles to enter the supreme leader's office and explode. The missiles obliterate the entire top floor of the building.

Nathan has a front-row seat to watch the explosion up close, safely, behind the most powerful shields of any ship in the galaxy. He doesn't even flinch from the initial explosion or from the debris flying at him that impacts the shields. He watches as the fireball curves around the shields in front of him. The flames seem to be performing a beautiful dance as they travel around the shields. Truly a unique thing to see.

Nathan turns and says, "Thank you, gentlemen, you can return your planes to the hangar deck now."

Nathan was so focused on the supreme leader he didn't even notice that his fighters are engaged with several squadrons of Xandurian fighters a few miles away.

Nathan jumps back into the little electric utility car and drives back to the island. After parking the car, he heads back inside to the elevators and takes one back up to the bridge.

Upon re-entering the bridge Nathan says, "CAG, bring the fighters home ASAP. It's time to leave."

"Aye sir."

"Tactical, activate the automatic anti-aircraft turrets."

"Aye sir, activating the triple-A turrets now."

The six squadrons of F-114 Tomcats head back to the carrier with what remains of the Xandurian fighters in pursuit. As the Tomcats start landing on the flight deck, the Xandurian fighters enter the virtual defensive sphere around the carrier that controls the triple-A turrets.

To say that the second-generation battle carrier has a lot of triple-A turrets would be a gross understatement. It has twice as many as the first-generation battle carrier and the new triple-A turrets have a higher rate of fire by a factor of three.

Two or three seconds after the Xandurian fighters come into range, the sky around the carrier seems to turn red from the number of laser blasts streaking up towards them. If that wasn't enough, the Aurora opens up with its triple-A turrets as well, and it has even more triple-A turrets than the Invincible. Needless to say, the Xandurian fighters don't last more than thirty seconds against the intense barrage coming at them.

It only takes about ten minutes to get all six squadrons of Tomcats back aboard the Invincible.

When the last fighter touches down on the flight deck the CAG says, "Admiral, all our fighters are back aboard."

"Any casualties, CAG?"

"Yes sir, we lost eight."

"Thank you, CAG, forward their names to me so I can write a message to their families."

"Aye sir."

"Okay, let's get out of here. Helm, take us back into orbit with the rest of the fleet."

"Aye sir, taking us up."

Mr. Bell nudges the ship straight up with the RCS thrusters until the ship is clear of the city, then he fires the main engines and climbs for orbit.

"Tactical, are the nanites programmed?"

"Aye sir, they've been programmed to perpetually seek out all Xandurian military technology and destroy it. We shouldn't ever have a problem with the Xandurians again."

"Excellent, thank you, Tactical."

It takes about five minutes for the two massive warships to climb back out of the atmosphere and enter orbit with the rest of the EDF fleet.

Once they achieve orbit, Nathan says, "Helm, disengage the anti-gravity generators."

"Aye sir."

"Comms, extend the bow long-range communications antennas."

"Aye sir."

"Tactical, return the forward shield harmonics to standard."

"Aye sir."

"Comms, open a channel to the fleet."

"Aye sir, channel open."

"Attention all commands, this is Admiral Stone. Arm all nano-missiles. Program them for an elevated air burst at a range of one mile above the surface. We are going to flood the planet's lower atmosphere with nanites and take out all of their military technology. You may fire when ready. Stone out."

Nathan presses a button on the command console on his chair to close the channel.

"Tactical, you may fire when ready."

"Aye sir, firing in 5… 4… 3… 2… 1… now."

Missiles fire and emerge from the launch tubes throughout the hull of the Invincible. Hundreds of missiles launched in all directions from the ship streak outward then turn towards the planet. Each of the three hundred and twenty or so EDF warships in orbit around Xandur launches its missiles.

Thousands of missiles fall towards the surface of the planet, each one targets a pre-programmed area ensuring complete coverage. When the missiles reach an altitude of one mile above the surface, there is a large puff of smoke from each missile as it breaks up into hundreds of small pieces with no explosion. The nanites have been released into the atmosphere all over the planet.

"Well, I say our job here is done. We have eliminated the Xandurian threat once and for all. It's time to head home. Don't you think, Mr. Bell?"

"I do indeed, Admiral."

"CAG, is the flight deck clear?"

"Aye sir, all fighters, equipment and personnel are safely back inside the ship."

"Excellent. Shut down the flight deck."

"Aye sir, shutting down the flight deck now."

"Comms, open a channel to the fleet."

"Aye sir, channel open."

"Attention all commands, this is Admiral Stone. Set course for home and engage your FTL drives, maximum speed. Stone out."

Nathan presses a button on the command console on his chair to close the channel.

"Helm, set course for home and engage the FTL drive, 14 TSL."

"Aye sir, course laid in, engaging the FTL drive, speed 14 TSL."

The huge battle carrier turns and accelerates rapidly away from the Xandurian home world. The bridge crew sees a bright blue flash of light through the bridge windows as the ship passes the speed of light.

"Tactical, verify that all other ships in the fleet have jumped with us."

Ms. Norata does a quick scan and says, "Aye sir, all other ships have jumped with us and are on course."

"Excellent, thank you, Tactical."

A minute later Mr. Bell says, "Admiral, we are on course for Earth and are traveling at 14 TSL. Estimated time of arrival is six days, fourteen hours and thirty-five minutes."

"Thank you, Helm, steady as she goes."

"Aye sir."

CHAPTER 13 – EDUCATING THE PRESIDENT

Six days later, the EDF fleet is about to arrive back home to Earth. It was an uneventful trip home, and for everyone, but Nathan, it was a relaxed trip. For the first time in a couple of years, Earth is not under threat of attack.

Nathan however, had something weighing on his mind the whole trip. Upon reaching Earth, he knows the president will summon him to London to report, in person, for a mission debrief. A meeting in which Nathan will have to inform the president that he disobeyed his direct order to wipe out the Xandurians.

Nathan has devised a plan to deal with the president, should he respond with threats of dismissal and court martial, but he is not an expert in dealing with politics and the law. He is an expert in war, tactics and the flow of battle. The president may have a few political or legal tricks up his sleeve to twist things in his favor. Nathan is going to treat the meeting as a battle, should things go badly, to try to keep the advantage on his side.

Nathan is on the bridge, sitting at his command station, when the fleet is approaching Earth.

Mr. Bell pipes up and says, “Admiral, we will be arriving back at Earth in one minute, sir.”

“Thank you, Helm, prepare to drop us out of FTL.”

“Aye sir.”

Nathan has always loved arriving back home to Earth. Dropping out of FTL, going from watching the stars streak by to instantly seeing that beautiful blue marble floating in a sea of black nothingness, all safe and sound, always makes him happy.

A minute later Mr. Bell says, “Arriving at Earth in 5… 4… 3… 2… 1… now.”

The battle carrier decelerates, and the bridge crew sees a bright blue flash of light through the bridge windows as the ship drops below the speed of light. Instantly, Earth appears through the front bridge windows.

“Helm, take us in and assume a standard orbit.”

“Aye sir.”

As the Invincible approaches Earth, the planet disappears on the port side of the ship, blocked by the huge flight deck. As the ship enters a high orbit around the planet, Nathan walks over to the port side bridge windows. He leans on the window ledge, waiting for what he refers to as ‘Earth rise’. That is the moment when the battle carrier banks to port to begin circling the planet and Earth rises above the edge of the flight deck and comes into view. He never tires of seeing that. On the bridge of a battle carrier is probably the only place a man can experience it, as a battle carrier is the only ship big enough to block the entire planet until they turn into orbit. It is a very similar experience to watching the sun rise from Earth.

A few minutes after the fleet has entered orbit around Earth, the communications officer says, “Admiral Stone, I have an incoming transmission from Earth, it’s the president, sir.”

“On screen please, Comms.”

“Aye sir.”

Nathan walks over to stand in front of his command station. The main view screen activates, and the president appears, sitting behind his large ornate wooden desk in his office in London.

“Welcome home, Admiral Stone. I assume your mission was a success?”

“Thank you, Mr. President, it was a complete success, sir.”

“That is truly great news, Admiral Stone. Why don’t you join me in my office in an hour for a full debriefing of the mission?”

“Very well, sir, I will see you in an hour. Stone out.”

Nathan walks back to his chair and presses a button on his command console to shut down the channel and the main view screen. He sits down in his chair to finish a few things when Ms. Norata walks over to speak with him.

“How do you think he’s going to react?”

“Like any slimy, egotistical politician that never had to pull a trigger and kill someone in his entire life. He’s going to accuse me of not blindly following his immoral, illegal orders.”

“You sound pretty certain.”

“Not my first rodeo, sweetheart.”

She smiles at hearing him call her sweetheart, especially in public. “Do you want me to come with you for moral support?”

“Mmmmm, no thank you. I think I’ll handle this alone. That way if it goes sideways, I take the blame and nobody else gets caught up in it.”

“Okay, good luck… sweetheart.”

The two exchange smiles and then Ms. Norata walks back over to her station.

Nathan gets up from his chair, looks at Mr. Black and says, “XO, you have the con. I’m taking a shuttle down to London to meet with the president, so you are in charge until I return.”

“Aye sir, I will take care of her until you return.”

Nathan walks to the back of the bridge and steps onto the elevator. He takes it down to the level for the battle carrier’s internal tram and takes a tram to shuttle bay alpha. Upon arriving in the shuttle bay, Nathan steps off the tram and walks over to one of the shuttles. He boards the shuttle, closes the door, jumps in the pilot’s seat, gets the shuttle ready and then radios for clearance to takeoff.

“Invincible air traffic control, this is Admiral Stone, requesting clearance for takeoff from shuttle bay alpha, port side.”

"Admiral Stone, this is Invincible air traffic control, clearance for takeoff granted, no traffic in the area, have a safe flight."

"Thank you, Invincible air traffic control. Lifting off."

Nathan pushes the throttles up a little and the shuttle lifts off the deck. He turns it ninety degrees to port and nudges it forward towards the huge landing bay doors. A few seconds later the shuttle passes through the landing bay's atmospheric force field and out into space.

Nathan gets on the radio again, "Earth space flight control, this is Admiral Nathan Stone, departing from the Invincible, requesting clearance for re-entry."

"Admiral Stone, this is Earth space flight control, clearance for re-entry granted, no traffic in the area."

"Thank you, Earth space flight control, beginning my descent."

Nathan noses the shuttle over and begins his descent into the atmosphere. In just a few short minutes he is over the Atlantic Ocean, approaching the west coast of England.

Nathan gets on the radio again, "London air traffic control, this is Admiral Nathan Stone, requesting an approach vector and clearance to land on the helipad on top of Earth World Council Tower."

"Admiral Stone, this is London air traffic control, transmitting approach vector now, clearance for a vertical landing on the helipad at Earth World Council Tower granted, no traffic in the area."

"Thank you, London air traffic control, approach vector received and laid in."

As Nathan approaches the Earth World Council Tower, he slows the shuttle down to a crawl and banks to starboard slightly to line it up with the helipad. Soon the shuttle is hovering at two hundred feet directly over the helipad. Nathan pulls back on the throttles and the shuttle descends slowly until it touches down.

Nathan shuts the shuttle down, opens the door, exits the shuttle, and walks across the short walkway towards the entrance to the building. Just as before, two British secret service agents meet him at the double glass doors and escort him down to the office of the president.

When they enter, the same woman, dressed in a red business suit this time, walks out from behind the desk with a tablet in her right hand. As she always does, she is holding the tablet pressed against her chest.

She approaches Nathan and says, "Admiral Stone, it's lovely to see you again, sir. If you will follow me, I will take you in to see the president."

"Very well, lead the way."

The woman takes him down the short hallway to the right of her desk. She knocks on the door, opens it, and walks in. Over her shoulder Nathan can see President Siebert sitting behind his large, antique, wooden desk.

The woman says, "Mr. President, I have Admiral Stone to see you, sir."

The president stands up and walks around in front of the desk while saying, "Yes, please come in, Admiral Stone."

Nathan reaches out to shake the president's hand and says simply, "Mr. President."

The two sit down in the armchairs in front of the president's desk, the president smiling and looking eager to find out how the mission went.

"So, tell me, Admiral, how did the mission go? Did you wipe out those blasted Xandurians?"

"The mission was a complete success, Mr. President. I doubt we'll have any more trouble from the Xandurians."

The expression on the president's face changed. The smile is now gone, and he looks puzzled.

"Can you explain that statement, Admiral Stone?"

"Of course, Mr. President. I sent a full battle group to each of the four planets that had a military base and a shipyard in orbit as outlined in the intelligence you provided to me. We nuked the bases on the surface from orbit and then wiped out the shipyards and the sentry ships using our laser cannons."

"Very well, go on, Admiral Stone."

"Next my battle group stopped on the way to Xandur to destroy the military space station and the sentry ships guarding it."

"Yes, go on, Admiral Stone."

"Our four battle groups rendezvoused at Xandur where we destroyed the sentry ships in orbit and blockaded the planet. I then took the Invincible and the Aurora into the planet's atmosphere where I wiped out their supreme leader and his generals."

"Oh, you did, did you?"

"Yes sir. After returning to orbit I had the fleet arm and fire every nano-missile in our arsenal at the planet, flooding the planet's atmosphere with nanites programmed to seek out all the Xandurian military technology and destroy it. The nanites will remain active in perpetuity and destroy any military technology they find any place on the planet."

At this point, the look on the president's face has changed to one of anger. His face has turned red, he stands up briskly, walks back behind his desk and sits down.

"Admiral Stone, am I to understand that you, on your own authority, did willfully, disobey a direct order from your commander-in-chief?"

"Yes, Mr. President, you understand perfectly."

"Do you have anything to say for yourself before I have you arrested and charged with insubordination?"

"I most certainly do, Mr. President. I refuse to commit genocide. If I had killed every man, woman and child on that planet, we would be no better than them. As I mentioned before, in a dictatorship, most of the population and even the military are forced to do things against their will under threat. I determined this to be the case on Xandur through my short conversation with their supreme leader. At that point it was my duty to remove the threat to Earth while protecting the innocent and helpless Xandurians, which I did."

"You can't be sure that you removed the threat to Earth."

"Yes, I can, Mr. President. The supreme leader was the driving force behind their aggression towards us. I took him and his military leaders out, I destroyed all military technology on the planet, I took out their shipyards and what remained of their fleet. How could they possibly be a threat to us anymore?"

"What if you're wrong, Admiral Stone? What if they have other military bases and shipyards out there that we don't know about?"

"Mr. President, wiping out the entire population on Xandur would not change the fact that there could be other bases and shipyards out there that we don't know about. If there are, then wiping out the entire population of Xandur would have given those Xandurians plenty of motivation to continue to attack Earth, only now it would be all the survivors seeking vengeance instead of one man's crazy delusion about ruling the galaxy."

"Neither one of us can, with a hundred percent certainty, say that we are right and the other is wrong. The fact of the matter is, Admiral Stone, you disobeyed a direct order from your commander-in-chief and for that, I hereby relieve you of your command. You will be taken into custody while you await court martial."

"Yeah, I don't think so, Mr. President. I don't think you've thought this through."

"What do you mean, Admiral Stone?"

"What I mean, Mr. President, is that genocide is a war crime. How do you think the president of Earth ordering the EDF fleet admiral to commit *THE* most heinous war crime ever devised by man will play out in the papers or in a courtroom? Can you be sure that none of this will blow back on you? Personally, I think you'd be finished if word of this was to get out."

Nathan can see by the look of shock and fear on the president's face that he gets it now. He just sits there staring at Nathan, not saying a word.

Nathan drives the point home. He sits forward in his chair with a menacing look on his face and says, "I have a number of friends that are news reporters that work for some pretty prestigious news outlets, some even owe me a few favors. So, if I even hear a whisper of charges being brought against me or any of my crew, I'll spill everything I know to the press so fast it'll make your head spin, you can count on that."

"You know you'd have made an excellent politician, Admiral Stone."

Smirking Nathan says, "Now now, there's no need for insults. I'd have to lower my IQ by about sixty points to qualify to be a politician, like you, Mr. President."

"Obviously I underestimated you, Admiral Stone."

"You're not the first man that has and I doubt you'll be the last, Mr. President. Do you know how I've stayed alive and have been so successful in my career? I never go into any situation without a tactical advantage. This combined with being righteous and honorable has kept me on the winning side for almost thirty years."

Nathan gets up out of his chair and walks towards the office door.

The president asks, "So what now then? How will we work together going forward?"

"Oh, you don't have to worry about that Mr. President. I'm going to retire from the EDF, for the second time in my career. You'll have my resignation and retirement papers in the next few days. You can inform Admiral Jameson that he can have his ship back. Goodbye, Mr. President, I hope I never have to see you again."

With that Nathan turns and walks out of the president's office. He is escorted back to the elevator and up to his shuttle on the helipad by the British secret service agents. He boards the shuttle, closes the door, jumps in the pilot's seat, gets the shuttle ready, and then radios for clearance to takeoff.

"London air traffic control, this is Admiral Nathan Stone, requesting clearance for a vertical takeoff from the helipad on top of Earth World Council Tower."

"Admiral Stone, this is London air traffic control, clearance for a vertical takeoff from the helipad at Earth World Council Tower granted, no traffic in the area."

"Thank you, London air traffic control. Lifting off."

Nathan pushes the throttles up a little and the shuttle lifts off the helipad. He turns it one hundred and eighty degrees and rams the throttles open. The shuttle blasts away from the tower, Nathan pulls the nose up and climbs rapidly.

Nathan gets on the radio again, "Earth space flight control, this is Admiral Nathan Stone, departing from Earth World Council Tower in London, requesting clearance for space flight."

"Admiral Stone, this is Earth space flight control, clearance for space flight granted, no traffic in the area."

"Thank you, Earth space flight control."

Several minutes after takeoff, the sky around the shuttle turns black as Nathan nears the edge of the planet's atmosphere. As he enters orbit, he spots the Invincible off in the distance and changes course towards her.

A few minutes later Nathan radios the Invincible, "Invincible air traffic control, this is Admiral Stone returning from Earth, requesting permission to land."

"Admiral Stone, this is Invincible air traffic control, you are cleared for landing in shuttle bay alpha, port side."

"Thank you, Invincible air traffic control."

As he approaches the battle carrier, Nathan lines the shuttle up with shuttle bay alpha from the port side. Nathan slows the shuttle as he nears the carrier and is soon passing through the atmospheric force field and into the bay. With a metallic clang, Nathan sets the shuttle down on the deck, powers it down, and opens the door.

As Nathan steps out of the shuttle into the bay, he is greeted by a saluting petty officer, a deckhand who has come to secure the shuttle, "Welcome back, Admiral Stone."

Nathan returns the salute, "Thank you, Petty Officer, carry on."

"Aye sir."

Nathan walks off across the bay heading towards the carrier's internal tram. Nathan boards the waiting tram and takes it to the stop for the island. When the tram stops, Nathan steps out onto the platform, walks over to the elevators, and takes one up to the bridge.

As Nathan steps out onto the bridge, the ship's computer announces in its female voice, "Admiral on the bridge."

Everyone stands and snaps to attention.

"At ease everyone."

Everyone takes their station again.

Nathan walks over and sits down in his command chair for a moment before he realizes he really has nothing to do other than go back to his stateroom to finish his resignation letter and retirement papers.

He is just about to stand up when Ms. Norata walks over and asks, "So, how did it go with the president?"

"Let's just say it went exactly how I thought it would and, in the end, he saw things my way."

The two smile at each other and then Nathan stands up to leave the bridge.

"How about you and the others join me in the officers' club for drinks at 19:00 hours tonight?"

"We'll be there... sweetheart."

Nathan smiles and walks towards the elevators at the back of the bridge, "XO, you have the con."

"Aye sir."

Nathan gets in the elevator and heads down to his stateroom to finish his resignation letter and retirement papers. When he is finished, he forwards them off to where they need to go and then packs the few belongings, he brought with him.

CHAPTER 14 – NATHAN'S NEW PLAN

At 18:45 hours, Nathan heads down to the officers' club. He wanted to arrive early to get a table near the windows and to order the first round of drinks. Nathan waits for the others to arrive, starring out the windows at the stars, the Earth and the other ships in orbit while enjoying a twenty-five-year-old single malt Scotch. The others walk in a few minutes later and sit down to find the first round of drinks has already arrived.

Nathan raises his glass and says, "To the best team in the EDF, and to well-executed plans."

They all clink their glasses together, say, "Here here," and take a sip of their drinks.

"As you all know, I went down to London earlier today for a meeting with the president to discuss how the mission went. As you can well imagine, he was none too happy that I disobeyed his direct order to wipe out the Xandurians. He threatened to relieve me of my command and have me court martialed for insubordination. I convinced him not to do that by pointing out that several reporter friends of mine would have a field day writing articles painting him as a genocidal maniac should he move forward. An image that would not sit too well with quite a number of his supporters."

Mr. Bell injects, "I wish I could have seen the look on his face when you said that."

With a little chuckle Nathan says, "It was priceless, Mr. Bell, absolutely priceless. The spineless little prick."

Mr. Black asks, "Are you going to be able to deal with him moving forward? After all, he is still your commander-in-chief and you will have to take orders from him."

"Actually, that won't be a problem moving forward. I submitted my resignation and my retirement papers this afternoon. As of tomorrow morning, I am officially retired... again. I only came back to the EDF because they needed me to take care of the Xandurian threat. I've done that."

Mr. Nagata asks, "So what will you do now?"

"Well to be honest, that will depend on the four of you."

Ms. Norata asks, "What do you mean, Nathan?"

"The five of us made a great team when we were with the Planetary Police. I was wondering if you all would like to be a team again?"

Mr. Bell asks, "Do you mean go back to the Planetary Police to help them rebuild."

"Well I thought about that, but honestly I originally went there to work with Carter, but now that he is gone, I really don't have much interest in that."

Mr. Black asks, "So what are we talking about then?"

"I'm talking about working for ourselves, doing our own thing."

Ms. Norata asks, "Doing what exactly?"

"Rescue and recovery. Maybe a little bounty hunting. We start our own company and we use our skills to rescue people that have been kidnapped, recover items that have been stolen, retake high jacked spaceships and such. We can work for ourselves, help people and make some pretty good money doing it."

Nathan looks around the table and sees that the four of them are intrigued at the idea. They were willing to follow him twice before, he's hoping they will want to follow him again.

Mr. Bell asks, "So if we were interested, how do we get started? We don't even have a ship. I don't know about the rest of you, but I don't have the kind of money you need to buy a spaceship. Where are we going to get the money to buy a ship?"

Nathan says almost hesitantly, "Actually... I already bought us a ship."

Ms. Norata asks, "You… you already bought us a ship? How could you afford that? I know they pay admirals well, but not *THAT* well."

"Well… yeah… that's true. I was wise with my money and invested a lot of it smartly," and then in a mumble he adds, "And… I come from a very wealthy family."

Mr. Black says, "I'm sorry, I didn't catch that last part. What did you say?"

"I said… I come from a very wealthy family."

Mr. Bell asks, "How come you've never told us this before?"

"It's not something I like to tell people. When you come from money, you learn not to tell people. That way you know their friendship is genuine and not financially motivated. Carter was the only one that knew. Although I am surprised that none of you figured it out."

Mr. Nagata asks, "And just how would we have figured that out?"

"Come on, you never wondered how I afforded a huge house in Jasper with my own hangar and helipad? How I afforded my car collection?"

Ms. Norata says, "I never gave it any thought."

"I know. None of you did. That's how I know that your friendships are genuine and that I can trust you."

Mr. Nagata says, "Okay, so enough about the money thing, let's talk about the ship. What kind of ship is it? How large is it? Do you have the technical specifications? I'd love to read up on it."

Nathan chuckles, "The ship will be delivered to my place in about a week. I'll send you what I have in the morning. Tonight, we are getting drunk and celebrating our new venture together. That is if you are all in."

Nathan looks at each of them, one by one and gets a nod from each of them, signaling that they're in.

"Excellent! Let's get another round of drinks, discuss all of you retiring from the EDF and talk about our futures together."

Nathan raises his glass and says, "To our future together."

They all clink their glasses together, say, "Here here," and take a sip of their drinks.

Nathan calls the waitress over and orders another round for the table. They spend the rest of the evening drinking and discussing their new venture. They all agree to submit their retirement papers to the EDF the next day and to meet at Nathan's house in Jasper in one week's time.

At the end of the night, when everyone is ready to retire for the evening, the waitress brings the bill over to the table.

Mr. Bell grabs the bill from the waitress and hands it over to Nathan, and says in very slurred speech, "I believe this is yours, Daddy Warbucks."

The whole table erupts in laughter, and everyone, but Nathan, gets up and walks away from the table, leaving Nathan shaking his head and pulling out his wallet.

The next morning, after treating his hangover, Nathan heads home to Jasper and spends the next few days and nights relaxing by himself, driving a few of his classic muscle cars, sitting on the deck by the fire drinking Scotch, and watching old science fiction movies at night.

On the fifth day, in the middle of the afternoon, the new ship is delivered. The delivery pilot sets it down on the helipad beside Nathan's house and then helps Nathan back it into his hangar. The delivery pilot takes Nathan through the entire ship, showing him how to operate the systems, to ensure that it was delivered as ordered, and to make sure Nathan is happy and satisfied with everything.

A few hours later, satisfied that it has arrived as he spec'd it out, Nathan signs off on the ship. A little while later, a helijet drops in to pick up the delivery pilot and takes him away.

Two days later, Ms. Norata, Mr. Bell, Mr. Black, and Mr. Nagata arrive at Nathan's house via helijet. Nathan is working in the hangar with the big hangar door open when the helijet lands. Nathan meets them just outside the hangar and before he can even say hello to them, Ms. Norata walks up throws her arms around him and kisses him passionately, catching Nathan off guard.

She breaks the kiss and says, "Hello, sweetheart. Did you miss me?"

"Yes, I certainly did, Baby."

Nathan looks up at Mr. Bell, Mr. Black and Mr. Nagata and sees that all three of them have a look of shock on their faces.

Mr. Bell is the first to ask, "Uh... guys, are we missing something here?"

Nathan says, "Yeah... ummm, we started seeing each other a few months ago."

The shocked looks on their faces slowly change to smiles.

Mr. Black says, "Good for you guys, we're happy for you."

Mr. Bell adds, "Yes, we're happy for you. Why didn't you tell us?"

Ms. Norata says, "Well it happened shortly after we found out Desiree was a cyborg and we didn't know how that would look. Then we ended up back in the military so we couldn't say anything."

Mr. Nagata pipes up and says, "All right, enough of the mushy stuff, let's get to this beautiful ship behind you."

Everyone laughs and they walk up the lower ramp into the ship.

Nathan says, “I think you’re all going to like this ship. I spec’d her out with all of you in mind.”

THE END

GLOSSARY

CAG – this is an acronym for Commander, Air Group. The CAG is responsible for all the embarked squadrons, their aircraft and their personnel aboard a battle carrier.

FTL – this is an acronym for "faster than light" and in this book refers to the fact that a ship is traveling faster than the speed of light and also to the engines / drive that propels a ship to speeds faster than the speed of light.

TSL – this is an acronym for "times the speed of light" and in this book is a reference to the speed a ship is traveling at. In several instances in this book you will see a ship's speed referred to as 14 TSL which is the top speed achieved by the latest and greatest FTL drive so far. It reads as 14 times the speed of light, but that is not quite accurate. The actual speed is 14^3 X the speed of light or 14 X 14 X 14 X the speed of light.

RCS – this is an acronym for "reaction control system" which is a spacecraft system that uses thrusters to provide attitude control, acceleration and braking.

DID YOU ENJOY THIS STORY?

If you answered yes to the question above, I would appreciate it if you could spend a couple of minutes and leave a review on the book's page wherever you bought it. I am a relatively new author, this is only the third book I have published, and positive reviews of my book will help bring it to the attention of other readers.

You can see my other titles at: **seanpatrickposey.com**

ABOUT THE AUTHOR

Sean Patrick Posey was born in Edmonton, Alberta, Canada in August of 1969 to parents Dave and Margaret Posey. Sean has two older brothers named Mark and Todd. Sean was hooked on science fiction at an early age. Some of his favorites include:

- Star Trek (TOS)
- Star Wars (original trilogy)
- Battlestar Galactica (TOS)
- Alien and Aliens
- Stargate Atlantis

Some of his other interests include classic 60s and 70s muscle cars, camping, fishing, martial arts, 3D computer animation and modeling, weightlifting and technology.

Sean graduated from the Northern Alberta Institute of Technology (NAIT) in 1992 earning his diploma in Computer Engineering Technology and has been an I.T. person for the last 27 years specializing in network design, installation and support.

Sean has two beautiful daughters from his first marriage named Alyssa and Sarah whom he loves dearly.

In January of 2017 he married the love of his life Nicole Hayman. Nicole is an American born in Los Angeles, but was living in St. Charles, Missouri when the couple met online. They spent 7 years in a long distance relationship before marrying and Nicole has now moved up to Edmonton to live with Sean.

Printed in Great Britain
by Amazon

39918332R00106